IRO
Bo
BUCKET LIST
By A. J. Harlem

A. J. Harlem

**BUCKET LIST: Text copyright © AJ Harlem 2020
All Rights Reserved**

With the exception of quotes used in reviews, this book may not be reproduced or used in whole or in part by any means existing without written permission from AJ Harlem.

Warning: The unauthorized reproduction or distribution of this copyrighted work is illegal. No part of this book may be scanned, uploaded or distributed via the Internet or any other means, electronic or print, without the author's written permission.

This book is a work of fiction and any resemblance to persons, living or dead is purely coincidental. The characters are productions of the author's imagination and used fictitiously.

Books by A. J. Harlem
Sin, Repent, Repeat
The Last Post
Blind Panic
Bucket List

Chapter One

The large rectangle photograph of a white-sanded beach, turquoise lapping waves, and a glossy palm tree could not be more opposite to the grey, dull doctor's office. To Mike Mendes it seemed as if life itself had been drained from the room. There wasn't even a wimpy spider plant on the sill or a homesick cactus on the desk.

Doctor Linnel was equally pallid. His cheeks were ashen—*I'm supposed to be the sick one*—his short bristly beard the colour of a dunked Digestive, and his tie, well, there was no way he should be wearing a black one.

Or maybe he should.

"So I really am sorry it's not better news." The doctor steepled his hands beneath his chin and shook his head. "These particular tumours, on the pancreas, are always buggers to deal with."

"Yeah. I get it." Mike nodded, his head seeming to wobble on his neck. He was struggling to let the words he'd just heard sink in.

"Are you sure you understand? Would you like me to go over anything else?" The doctor picked up a pen and tapped it on a notepad. "Obviously there will be a letter in the post summarising our discussion, but I don't want anything in it to be a surprise."

"No, I know what you've told me. Terminal, right?"

The doctor slow-blinked and inclined his head. "We prefer incurable these days."

"Is there a difference?"

"I suppose not, just doesn't sound so...about to happen."

"But it will." Mike sighed at the vanishing of his dream to go and live back in Portishead by the sea. Get a bungalow with a woman he'd yet to meet but was sure would have an insatiable sex drive and curves to die for.

He huffed at that.

To die for.

Well, as it happened…

"We had, of course, hoped chemotherapy would be more effective, and if it hadn't been for the complication of—"

"It's okay, Doctor. I know you did your best."

Doctor Linnel smiled sadly. Oh, how Mike had come to hate those sympathetic lip stretches. He'd seen them on the women who'd taken his blood, the nurses in the chemo-lounge, the radiographer, and Mrs Robin over the road—telling the daft old cow and seeing the expression on her face had made his mind up not to tell any of his other neighbours. At six-feet-three, and an ex-boxer, Mike couldn't stand to be thought of as weak, and that something—the Big C—had got the better of his strong, powerful body.

"Can I give you some advice?" Dr Linnel asked.

"Of course." Mike cleared his throat. "I'll take whatever I can at this stage."

Another sad smile as he leaned forward. "Obviously I don't have a crystal ball, but I'd estimate you have another two or three months of feeling well, Mike."

"And after that?" There'd been no Pearly Gates for Mike. Not after what he'd done all those years ago to that woman he'd happened across in Ealing Woods. It had been unexpected fun and wholly satisfying, but had it been worth the years of worrying that her body would be dug up and newfangled technology would pin her murder on him? Maybe it was that low-grade stress, the permanent looming threat of prison that had given him the damn cancer? His crime had literally eaten away at him.

"When you can't cope at home," the doctor was saying, "and your pain needs round-the-clock management, Ironash Hospice will be a safe and welcoming place for you."

"Hospice." That word hung in the air. Funny that it started with the same letter as happy, healthy, and horny.

It's only small, but the staff are excellent and very experienced. You do not have to fear a painful, undignified death."

"I wouldn't want that." Mike squeezed his eyes shut. At the mention of death an image of *her* flashed in his brain. Neck twisted unnaturally, her skin bloody, bruised, and dirt-strewn from the woodland floor. Eyes open, staring forever without seeing, and lips parted in a silent scream. If he'd had a camera he would have risked a photograph before he'd popped her in a deep-as-he-could-dig-with-his-hands grave. But sadly he hadn't, it was just a memory.

"If it were me sitting where you are." Doctor Linnel nodded at the photograph of the beach. "I'd get myself somewhere you've always wanted to go."

"A holiday?"

"Yes, if that's what you fancy. See things you've always wanted to see, try food you've never tried, experience as much as you can while you can. Some people call it a bucket list." He chuckled softly. "I've never known why."

"Things to do before you kick the bucket, I suppose." Mike shrugged.

"Oh, I've never thought of it like that." His eyebrows rose, and he smiled. "I reckon you're right. Anyway, if I were you, I'd make the most of feeling well for the time being and tick off the things on your bucket list."

Mike stared at the sand and waves. The doctor had a point. Maybe it was time to take a holiday, feel the sand beneath his toes, sip pina colada at sun set and watch pretty girls in their bikinis.

But that will mean getting a passport.

Something he hadn't done since *her*.

He'd watched a movie once. A serial killer had been caught when going through passport control. The authorities, huge stern men, had homed in on the guilty bloke who hadn't stood a chance at running. It was a movie scene that had played over and over in Mike's head in the form of sweaty nightmares.

He stood. Irritated that *she'd* stopped him from getting that passport and seeing the world.

"Bitch," he muttered.

"What was that?" the doctor asked with a frown and also standing.

"Er...itch. You know, where the chemo line was." He rubbed his arm. "Skin's a bit sensitive."

"Should settle down soon." The doctor held out his hand.

Mike took it and shook. The man was small, his bones fragile. Likely he'd never even smelt a gym, let alone been in one.

"Make everyday a great day," the doctor said. "We should all do that anyway, but now, Mike, you really have to obey that rule. Don't hold back on what makes you feel good, what gives you that buzz. Take it by the horns and don't let go."

"I'll remember that. Thank you." Mike touched the rim of the baseball cap he used to cover his now wispy hair and walked to the door.

'Don't hold back on what makes you feel good.'

He would do just that. Take control of this shitty situation. Maybe even get himself on a bus to Portishead and wander along the coast. Better still, take a walk to Ealing Woods and see if he'd get lucky again. Stranger things happened, and right now, fate did seem to be hurling some weird crap his way.

Mike took the number ten back to the Wilton Estate and disembarked a stop earlier than usual so he could detour along the canal.

It was the end of August, the wildflowers had grown too eagerly and now had stems so long they wilted over the towpath towards the water's edge, white-flowered heads bobbing. The hedgerow was crammed full of nettles and dandelions. Small black bugs swarmed in plumes, and Mike batted them away as he walked past the sight of a murder scene.

A month or so ago, an old fisherman had been sitting waiting for a bite, and Roy Campbell, a local simpleton, had taken it upon himself to drown him. It had been the talk of the town. Roy had been on a rampage, murdering two other old biddies in the process. Bloody idiot had been easy to catch, though. He'd had a bang to the head, so the local paper said, so had no common sense to take action against being caught.

Mike had laughed when he'd read the article. The police of Ironash had hardly even had to work to apprehend the fool. He'd all but left a trail of breadcrumbs, and now the moron would spend the rest of his days rotting in prison.

Prison.

A word that sent a shiver up Mike's spine whenever he heard it or even thought of it. Sure, he was a big bloke, but in *there*, that made you more of a target—a conquest, an achievement if you could be knocked out and bones broken.

Mike watched a pair of Mallards land on the water then stooped and picked up a stone. He chucked it their way, tutting when it missed the female.

Prison. The whole idea wasn't so scary now. It was as if a weight had been lifted from his shoulders. More than a weight, a ton of rubble that had been squeezing his chest, suffocating him for years, had gone.

He inhaled deep, the warm air filling his throat and lungs. He was a free man, and he always would be. Chances of them finding *her* before he carked it were slim to none. And even if they did, they could sentence him to one hundred years and he'd still only do a few months.

He carried on walking. What a strange feeling; it was like a real sensation stroking over his skin, caressing him. He hadn't realised what a burden the threat of prison had been. All these years, playing in his subconscious like a tape recorder on repeat, there'd been fears of being gang raped and humiliated or cut with razors hidden in soap, beaten and left for dead in a damp, grimy corner.

"I am a free man," he said, setting down his shoulders, "and I have the power."

And he did feel powerful. Like nothing could really hurt him anymore. Well, the Big C could, and it would, but nothing else really mattered.

Perhaps that was why people on death's door jumped out of planes, swam with sharks, or bungee jumped. Their 'avoid death' switch was no longer working. Death was walking towards them anyway, fast, footsteps loud. You couldn't be scared of getting sick once you were sick, it had happened. Just like you couldn't be scared of dying when it was on this year's calendar.

So what should he do with this feeling of power?

Mike wasn't sure, and turning away from the canal towards home, he pondered again on the idea of getting a passport. Probably he should just risk it and hope for the best. Yeah, he'd do that. Tomorrow he'd wander up to Tesco, they had a photo booth there. He'd get some pictures taken, organise that passport.

The ice-cream van meandered past, its annoying tune screaming from a speaker and scratching his eardrums.

"Fucker," Mike muttered. He hated the ice-cream van. Should be banned. A public disturbance, that was what it was. Not only was it an old diesel thing that polluted Ironash, when it stopped, all the little sods on the street rushed out and kept it there, engine chugging over. Right outside his bloody house, too. Impossible to ignore. Almost worth hoping for rain so it didn't appear.

Mike shoved his hands into his jeans pockets. He'd cook himself a steak tonight. Since he'd finished chemo, his appetite had come right back, and there was no point scrimping on food now. He'd eat whatever the hell he fancied. Caviar and champagne if that tickled his balls, why not. He had a credit card, might as well max that out.

Oh yes, the credit card, now that made the possibilities for his bucket list endless. He was rich, he'd never have to pay the bastard off.

Chuckling, he walked past Mrs Robin's garden. His mirth died, though. Her garden brought down the tone of the street. It was full of ugly gnomes in an assortment of grotesque poses.

Mike's nan had collected gnomes, too. She'd been a total bitch. Quick to clout him around the ear and mean when it came to dishing out food. She'd had a foul mouth on her, too, and slagging him off to anyone who'd listen seemed to be a hobby of hers. She did it in English and Portuguese. She was originally from Lisbon. He was the only one around here who understood the vile things she said in her mother tongue.

Mike's mum, a single mother, had vanished into the sunset with a new boyfriend when Mike was eight, so he'd had no choice but to live with his nan. She'd had no choice but to take him in.

It had been a relief when she'd croaked. Mike had been eighteen and two days. There was hardly anyone at her funeral. Not surprising really. She had more gnomes than friends.

A car drew up. Mike slowed, his attention caught.

A woman got out. Tammy, her name was. Mrs Robin's daughter. She reminded Mike of *her*—long legs, big boobs, and fluffy hair. Except Tammy was a smiler, always ready to call hello and wave. *She* hadn't smiled. *She* had begged and pleaded and screamed. He'd never had one smile from *her*.

"Hi, Mike, how are you?" Tammy said, leaning back into the car and presenting her round, jean-clad arse.

"Fine."

She straightened, holding a bright-red handbag dotted with silver studs and leather tassels hanging from it. "Nice day again." She shut her car door and clicked the key fob. It flashed and beeped.

"Yeah, it is." He nodded at the house. "Your mum keeping well?"

"As well as can be expected at her age and a widow." Tammy yanked the strap of her bag over her shoulder. A tight blue t-shirt showed off her cleavage and hugged her big tits.

Are they real?

Mike licked his lips.

"I visit every day," she said with a shrug. "But you probably know that, my car is always here."

"Yeah, I've noticed."

"Work going okay?" she asked.

That question surprised him. Had he ever discussed his work with her?

"Er, I suppose. Pays the bills."

"What is it you do again?"

He struggled not to stare at her right breast. A tiny black bug had landed right over the nipple. She hadn't noticed.

"I'm a translator. Portuguese."

"Oh, you're fluent then."

"Yeah, my grandmother, she was from Lisbon."

She spotted the bug and batted it away. "Oh, I'd love to go there, I'm sure it's beautiful."

Mike smiled. He'd never been, and in all honesty, it was the last thing on his list of things to do. If the language reminded him of his bitch of a nan, then going to her birthplace would bring back a cauldron of memories.

"Well, I should get going." She stepped past him, a waft of sweet, powdery perfume filling the air. "Take Mum her sandwich. You have a nice day, Mike."

"And you."

She walked up the front path, past the gnomes, and let herself in with a key. "Hi, Mum. It's only me."

When the door shut, Mike shifted from one foot to the other. Tammy was small and light; he'd bet she wouldn't weigh much despite those tits. And she smelt good, too. He wished he could inhale her scent properly. Bury his nose in her soft hair, lick her neck, squeeze her arse, put his...in her...

Damn, now wouldn't that be nice. It had been so long.

He crossed the road, adding to the top of his bucket list: *Get a Woman*.

Chapter Two

"I thought you were going out with Ben?" Shona's mum said, glancing up from her glossy magazine.

They were seated in the back garden, beside the buddleia which was alive with tortoiseshell butterflies.

Shona checked her phone. "Yes, he's picking me up in an hour." She finished the last of her lemonade. "I suppose I should get ready."

"Where are you going?"

"I'm not sure." She stood. "But I bet he's organised something nice, he usually does."

"This is your fifth date with him," her dad said. "When do we get to meet him properly?"

She laughed. "Soon. I don't want to scare him off."

"We're hardly scary." Her mum laughed.

"You're not, Mum." She bent and kissed her father's cheek. "But this one…"

"What does that mean?" he asked, looking indignant.

"I fear you may think you're back in the interrogation room."

"Can you blame me for being protective?"

"Not at all. But let me settle into our relationship for a while longer. It's the first time…"

The truth was, this was the first time Shona had wanted any kind of relationship with a bloke other than friend, family, or professional. Since that night, all those years ago, she hadn't been able to think of romance or dating.

But Ben had come into her life at a point in time when she was ready and able to put the past behind her. Or at least that was what she hoped.

"I think you're right to take it slow," her mother said. "It certainly can't hurt."

"We're both busy people, and he doesn't seem to be in any rush. He's not pushing, so it suits."

"Have you told him your history?" Her mother dropped her reading glasses to dangle from the chain at her neck.

"No." Shona paused. "But I know I need to."

"Only when you're ready. And if he's as nice as he seems to be, he'll understand."

"I agree, and I think he's sensed that I'm taking a while to get into this whole dating thing."

"I would imagine he can't believe his luck," her father grumbled. "A beautiful woman like you, successful, intelligent, *and* single. You're his lottery win."

She laughed. "You say the nicest things."

"I try." He grinned suddenly.

"But I really should get ready now."

An hour later, Shona was hanging around the front door waiting for Ben to arrive. She'd nip straight out and jump in his car, save any introductions having to be made.

She checked her phone. There was a message from Earle.

Went back to the office and finished off last week's paperwork. Hope you're having a good weekend.

She replied 'thank you' with a sigh. Earle really should have left it until Monday. They'd had a busy week—though not as busy as some—and paperwork from several minor cases had stacked up. But it could have waited until they were back on the clock.

The sound of an engine rumbled from the driveway.

"Bye, Mum, bye, Dad," she called, grabbing her keys from the side cabinet.

Her father appeared so fast it was as if he'd been lurking around the hallway corner.

"You're off then." He opened the front door before she could reach it.

"Yes. I'll see you later."

He didn't appear to be listening. Instead, he was craning his neck to see Ben in his car.

Luckily, he was parked behind three other cars on the long drive so not quite in view.

"Soon, Dad." She kissed his cheek. "I promise I'll introduce you soon."

He frowned. "I'd prefer to get to know the man you're seeing right about now."

"You didn't worry when I was in London."

"That was different."

"Why?"

"For one, I knew you weren't dating, and two, you weren't living under my roof. I couldn't panic every time you stepped out the door because I didn't know you were going out."

"Ignorance is bliss, eh?"

He huffed.

"But you're forgetting one important thing." She stepped past him.

"What's that?"

"I'm a black belt now." She grinned.

"Yeah, but so is he." He frowned and pointed at the driveway.

"You worry too much."

"It's my job." His frown smoothed, and he held up his hand. "Have a nice time."

"Thank you. I have a key, so don't wait up."

"Of course I will."

Shona hurried down the drive and jumped into Ben's white BMW. She slammed the door. "Unless you want third-degree interrogation from my father, we should get out of here."

He laughed. "You don't think I could handle it?"

"I didn't say that." She smiled. "But it's not ideal for a Saturday night."

"Gotcha." He put the car in reverse, then set his arm around the back of her seat so he could twist and look over his shoulder.

His aftershave filled the car, and his dark hair appeared a little damp as though he'd just jumped through the shower.

"Where are we going?" she asked as he went backwards.

"There's a canal-side pub, about three miles away, nice garden. Thought we'd eat outside as the sun is shining." He turned, and after lingering his attention on her for a moment, he faced forward and drove away. "You look nice. I like your dress."

"Thank you." She smoothed the soft, pale-green cotton over her legs.

"But if it gets cold, we'll go inside."

"I'm sure it won't. We're having a great summer."

"We are." He smiled at her again. "The best."

She knew what he was implying. It was great that they'd met. And it was, she agreed with his sentiment. But mainly it was great that she'd put three evil men behind bars who'd attacked her and her two friends when they were teenagers. It was also great because she'd returned to Ironash not full of fear but full of victory. And that meant both she—and Tina—could move on.

Tina was doing well. Shona visited her weekly, and on the last trip to see her they'd walked in the hospital grounds together. Tina's confidence was growing. She was getting mentally stronger, more confident. The doctors were thrilled with the change in her behaviour since news of the arrests.

Soon they arrived at The Tricky Fox Inn. Built of gingerbread-coloured stone, it was dripping with stunning hanging baskets. The garden was set against the wide, still canal. Huge red umbrellas provided some shade from the evening sun over the wooden tables. There was a low hum of conversation, and the scent of chips made her stomach rumble.

"This is nice." Shona took a seat at a table farthest away from other diners.

"I'm glad you like it. My sister and her husband came here a few weeks ago. She recommended it."

Shona smiled and took a menu. "How is married life suiting her?"

"Very well." He leaned forward, his eyes flashing. "I'm not supposed to say anything for another week, but she's expecting a baby."

"Oh, congratulations. Uncle Ben, it suits you."

He chuckled. "No it doesn't, I sound like some kind of rice-based microwave meal."

Shona laughed. "Perhaps go with Uncle B then."

"I might have to. You won't say anything, though. Not until she's made the official announcement."

"Of course not. But thanks for telling me, I'm thrilled for her."

"Me, too. It's what she's always wanted." He nodded at the bar. "What would you like to drink?"

"White wine, please."

"Coming right up."

As the sun set, Shona enjoyed a fish-and-chip meal almost as much as Ben's company. He was always so easy to chat to, had a quick smile, and seemed genuinely interested in her as a person.

"So tell me about your childhood," she said, setting her knife and fork down. Her plate was clear.

"Not much to tell."

"I'm sure there is. Where did you and your sister grow up?"

"We were in Yorkshire until I was fifteen and she was sixteen." He paused and looked out at the canal. A set of ripples shimmied over the surface. A boat had just passed. "And then we came to Ironash."

"Really? Odd timing. You must have been in the throes of exams."

He shrugged and reached for his drink. "Yes, but you know...we had to move."

"Why?"

He took a sip, his eyelids a little heavy.

Shona waited for him to go on.

"Just...you know, things." He paused. "We couldn't stay in Yorkshire anymore. Mum didn't want to."

"She didn't like it?"

"I suppose that's what happened." He set down his empty cola glass. "But Ironash has been good to us, plus my mum's brother is here. He owns the estate agents I work at."

"Yes, you mentioned that before. A real family business."

"It is. And I've got the dojo up and running, which was a dream of mine, so that's a big achievement."

"It is on top of a day job."

"It takes up a lot of time." He set his hand over hers. "Time I'd rather be spending with you."

She smiled and enjoyed the warmth from his skin. "Well, lucky for you, I enjoy the dojo, too, so it's a win-win."

* * * *

Monday morning kicked off with a heavy dousing of rain that drenched the streets of Ironash.

Shona dashed from her car into Ironash Police Station and tried to avoid the puddles and keep her umbrella from turning inside out. She wasn't particularly successful, and when she pushed through the door, her plain blue slacks were dotted with water and her umbrella had one spoke sticking at an odd angle.

"Good morning, ma'am," Darren said, looking up from the reception desk.

"It is?" She dropped her brolly into a holder. "I know we need some rain, but really, the tap has been turned on full."

"Farmers and gardeners will be glad of it."

She ran her hand over her hair. "I suppose so. Anything happening?"

"No, all quiet. We had our run of it last month, what with the Campbell, Umbridge, and Napier cases."

"Yes, it's true what they say, things come in threes, and that includes serial killers."

He shuddered. "We've had enough of them in our small town."

"I agree."

"Earle's here."

"Ah good."

"He may have been here all weekend." Darren tutted. "His car was there when I went on Friday and in the same spot when I got here an hour ago."

She frowned. Why would Earle come into work early on a Monday morning? Bad enough that he gave up his Saturday afternoon to finish off their paperwork.

She ambled up the stairs, saying hello to a few colleagues as she went.

When she reached the large open-plan office, Earle was bent over a file on his desk, intense concentration etched on his face.

Shona headed straight for the coffee machine and made them both a cup. After wandering over, she set one on top of a coaster with a picture of a yellow cupcake and the words *I'd Rather Be Baking*. "Morning, partner."

"Oh, hi." He smiled. "Didn't see you arrive."

"You're busy with something."

"It's nothing really." He pushed the file to one side and reached for his coffee. "Thanks."

Shona retrieved a muesli bar from her desk drawer and unwrapped it. "What time did you arrive here?"

He shrugged. "I dunno. About seven."

"Seven. On a Monday morning when there's nothing going down."

He sipped his coffee. "I couldn't sleep. Thought I'd get a head start."

"Nothing to get a head start on."

"There's always things. Minor thefts in the town, one-zero-one calls that need following up."

"Like missing gnomes." Shona grinned. She shouldn't tease him about his not-so-secret admirer, Tammy Robin, but it was hard not to.

"Yep, that sort of thing." He paused. "You want me to do a search on Ben Thomas?"

"What?" She raised her eyebrows. Where had that come from?

"I was just thinking, at the weekend, you know. Maybe we should dig a little."

"Maybe we shouldn't, that's an abuse of police resources and an invasion of privacy."

"I bet your dad would if he was here."

"And I would tell him the same thing as I'm saying to you, no."

"Wouldn't take Andy long."

"No."

"Okay, I was just saying, before you get serious with him. Make sure he's not a weirdo or serial killer." He nodded at the window. "Cats and dogs out there."

"Tell me about it." She sighed and sat at her desk. She supposed she should be grateful the men in her life were protective, but she'd worked hard to be able to protect herself. Not only that, she considered the mutual respect she and Ben had for each other to be precious. How would she be able to look him in the eye knowing she'd had a dig around in his history? And what the hell would she do if there was something there?

"Andy added to your FYI pile on Saturday," Earle said.

"He was in, too?"

"Yeah, said he had a few searches that needed extra attention."

Shona didn't believe that for a second. Andy was going through a rough time with a divorce and the recent loss of his stepfather. Chances were he'd simply wanted a place to go and something to do, the same as Earle had.

Not that Shona would say that out loud. Earle was touchy about his situation, had been ever since that shooting in Manchester when his ex-partner had taken a couple of bullets. One minute he was worried sick about him, the next he didn't want to know—so long as he was alive. Shona had been foolish enough to mention he visit Patrick. That had resulted in a head-snapped-off moment. She hadn't brought the subject up again.

But the detective in her was curious. There was this need to know that she simply couldn't deny. Earle's private business, however, was not *her* business, so she kept the gnawing inquisitiveness caged as best she could.

"Napier sentencing appearance has been set," Earle said.

"Oh, when for?"

"Next month."

"That's quite soon, considering."

"What do you think he'll get?"

"Three murders and one attempted." She finished her muesli bar. "Blind or not, he can expect twenty-five, perhaps longer."

"Hopefully much longer."

"I agree." She shook her head. "To think I went around to his place to protect him from an attacker, yet he was the one doing the attacking."

"Just goes to show you can never…" Earle stared over Shona's right shoulder, at the entrance to the open-plan office. His eyes widened, and he swallowed. "What the hell?"

Shona turned.

Standing beside Darren was a woman in a bottle-green raincoat. She had dark hair piled high with two loose sections hanging over her ears. Her face was perfectly made up with long dark lashes and bright-red lipstick.

Shona swung her attention back to Earle. Despite his black skin, she was sure he'd paled.

"Who is that?" she asked quietly as Darren pointed their way then stepped forward with the woman.

"That," Earle said, "is Patrick's wife."

Chapter Three

Mike let himself into his house, still thinking about getting a woman. It would take some doing. Not that he'd fallen out of the ugly tree, he was okay-looking, but he'd never had the gift of the gab that other blokes seemed to have. Conversations with girls soon ran dry. It was as if he was on a different wavelength to them. Hardly surprising, really, they spoke in riddles, never actually saying what they actually meant or wanted.

Stupid cows.

He shut the door, flicked the lock, and secured the chain. Habit. Then, as was his routine, he checked the three downstairs rooms were exactly as he'd left them.

The living room had a big bay window with heavy nets his nan had chosen years ago. They'd yellowed over time. The brown corduroy sofa cushions were plump despite being old and the coffee table clutter free. A picture of woodland, on a gloomy night, hung over an armchair that faced a small television. Beneath the TV a blue-and-white football scarf—FC Porto—had been carefully draped.

He moved to the next room. A skinny-legged dining table with black chairs stood in the centre. A tall cabinet with glasses that were no way near precious enough to be displayed towered next to the window. The curtains, red striped, were closed. He had to keep them this way. Couldn't afford anyone nosing in.

"Hey, you little pricks," he said, frowning at the five garden gnomes standing in the corner. "You haven't got long left with me, another few months at the most." He laughed, though the sound grated on his throat. "Bet that's pleased you, hasn't it. You'll be free when I'm dead, to go back to Mrs Robin's garden and grin dumbly at everyone who passes by."

He shut the door with a slam. He hated the gnomes so he'd taken them whenever the opportunity had arisen over the last six months.

Trouble was, he'd been stuck with them then. He had no way of getting rid of them. Couldn't exactly put them out with the rubbish on a Friday. And with no car, walking backwards and forwards with them to Ealing Woods and dumping them was too much hassle.

He'd considered getting a car but didn't want the expense. Besides, he hadn't driven for five years, not since that accident. Bloody woman with a car full of kids had been in the middle of the road turning right. Wasn't his fault it had been foggy and he hadn't seen the Volvo until the last minute.

So no, he was stuck with the gnomes, but at least he had a spare room to keep the bastards in. He didn't have to stare at their ugly mugs all the time.

He went into the kitchen and flicked the kettle on. Staring out of the window, he checked that all was as it should be in the rear garden. Yep, the vegetable patch was in sunshine, the cut-n-grow lettuce coming on nicely, along with the runner beans on their poles.

While the kettle boiled, he went up the stairs. It was strange. He was dying. He was on his last few sunrises and sunsets, yet he felt absolutely fine. If the doctor hadn't told him anything was amiss, he'd have thought the chemo had done its job and he was back on track.

Yet, the appointment had told another story—the universe had different plans for him.

'You have another two to three months of feeling well.'

It really wasn't long. A blink in time.

A familiar anger at the unfairness of it all welled as he opened the door to his office. On his desk sat his computer and his current translation job in the form of a book. The anger grew, his blood heated. He picked up the book and flung it at the wall. It bounced off, just missing him as it crashed to the floor.

"Fucker!" He kicked it, hard, the pages wrinkling under the toe of his boot. "Why me?"

It had been a question he'd asked himself many times. He knew the answer really...just didn't like to admit it. But now he'd have to. He'd have to face the truth that he was paying for his crime.

He'd taken a life.

Now his was being taken as payback.

And it was all *her* fault. Silly bitch. Why had she been in the woods that day? All pretty, delicate, and weak. Perhaps if she'd put up more of a fight he'd have spooked and let her get away. Then this wouldn't be happening.

He went to the box room at the back of the house. In it was a single bed with a black metal frame. It used to be his, when his nan was alive. But now the blue-dotted duvet cover had been replaced with a pink flowery one. Just in case his mother ever needed a place to stay.

Just in case she came back. For him.

"Who am I kidding?"

It had been decades since he'd seen her. Was she even alive? Perhaps the new boyfriend had done her in when they'd taken a romantic stroll in the woods. Maybe that was why she'd never returned. She was rotting under leaves and mulch, worms wriggling around her decaying bones, through her eye sockets and pelvis.

That kind of thing did happen, after all.

He studied the metal headboard, and a sudden image of a naked woman lying on the bed popped into his imagination—a woman who was there just for him, for his pleasure, for him to act out all his desires and finally, get satisfaction that wasn't from his own hand.

She was like *her*, this woman in his mind. Curvy and blonde, long legs, voluptuous and tanned.

He stepped up to the bed and rattled the metalwork. It was a sturdy bed and it would hold someone being chained to it.

Chained to it.

He blew out a breath, and there was a familiar stirring down below.

Yeah, that was what he wanted. No, make that *needed*. And as it was top of his bucket list and he was short on time, he'd take action as soon as possible.

He picked up a small brass key he kept on the sill and locked the window. He pocketed the key and drew the blackout blind down. Might as well start getting the room ready for the new *her*.

Feeling as though he'd found a silver lining on his dark cloud of death, Mike made a cup of tea. He then sat at his computer, ignoring emails that were to do with work, and went straight to Amazon. Within minutes he was filling his virtual shopping basket.

Samsung forty-three inch, high-def, crystal, smart TV.

Oak TV stand.

Leather recliner—heated and with massage function.

Gourmet luxury food hamper.

Ultimate collection of fine wines.

Whisky gift box.

Viper TACTICAL—professional heavy duty police handcuffs, nickel-plated steel with two keys individually serial numbered.

Silicone ball gag.

When he clicked BUY NOW, a surge of adrenaline entered his bloodstream. It was so much money, and all on his credit card. His debt would have to die with him.

He laughed.

What else could he buy? He'd have to have a think.

But not for too long, he didn't have time on his side.

Good thing the cuffs and gag were on Prime and were arriving the very next day.

* * * *

"Thanks." Mike took the parcel from the postie. In the thin hours of dawn he'd woken with a fever, imagining the box to be spilling its contents on his doorstep for all to see. He'd be found out, his plan scuppered before he'd even got the show on the road.

And that would never do.

But luckily, it had only been a dream and the box was secure.

He rushed into the living room and spilled out the contents, checking the cuffs' strength—perfect—and trying the ball gag for himself. All he could do was concentrate on breathing when it was in, and talking was impossible. He managed a bit of a shout-cry, but nothing that would be heard by neighbours. He was in a detached house, thank goodness.

He put the cardboard packaging in the recycle bin out the back. A noise to his right caught his attention. He studied the silver birch tree that had grown from a sapling to a monster in his lifetime.

Meow

His gaze went higher. And then he saw it. About halfway up was a fluffy grey cat. It belonged to the man behind him, the one who played his music too loud whenever the sun came out and everyone else wanted to enjoy their garden.

"Stupid thing," he muttered. "I'm not helping you. You'll have to get down the way you went up."

He tutted and walked back to the house.

It was then the idea came to him. It was almost like running into a wall, it hit him so fast.

The cat was the perfect lure.

Quickly, he went to the living room window and peeked out of the nets. Mrs Robin's house was as he'd expected and had Tammy's car parked outside.

She hadn't left.

Yet.

A glance at the clock told him she'd be going soon, within the next ten minutes or so. She always did. An hour and a half with her mother each day was her routine.

What a good daughter.

He shifted from one foot to the other, anticipation gripping his stomach and shooting up his heart rate. His mouth dried, and a tingle went up his spine and over his scalp.

He hadn't felt that since he'd been in the woods and seen *her*.

While he waited, he checked out the rest of the quiet street. Most people were at work. Mrs Robin was unusual in that she was in all day. The majority of the occupants were young professionals, and even if they had kids both parents were working to make ends meet.

He scratched his arm, where the long-line had gone in for his chemo. It stung, the skin was red and irritated. He hadn't lied to the doctor about it itching.

"Come on. Where are you?" he muttered.

He'd have to act fast when he saw her. There was no time for messing about. Luckily, he had his boots on ready.

And then the red door pulled open.

Tammy appeared, blonde hair as fluffy as clouds and her tasselled bag over her shoulder.

With his pulse thudding in his ears, Mike rushed to his own front door and unleashed the chain. He opened it and jogged down the path.

"Hey, Tammy."

She paused by her car, key fob poised, and looked up. "Oh, hi, Mike. Everything okay?"

Mike came to a halt on the kerbside and downturned his mouth. "No, not really?"

"Why?" Her smooth brow furrowed.

"There's a cat, stuck up the tree in my garden." He tried to inject as much concern as possible into his tone. "And it's been there for so long. I don't know what to do."

"Oh dear." She took a step towards him. "How high up is it?"

"About ten feet, maybe more." He glanced back at the house, feigning desperate worry. "Perhaps you'll come and see it, try and coax it back to earth." He gestured down his body. "Poor little thing is scared of a big brute like me."

"Well, I—"

"It really is very scared. Won't stop meowing."

She nibbled on her bottom lip.

"In fact, I think it's a kitten," he went on, "it's so frightened. Wants its mum, see."

"A kitten. Oh no. Come on then, show me."

Mike held in a smile even though it made his cheeks ache to not let it out. "Great, thank you. This way."

They hurried down his garden path together, then he gestured for her to go inside first. "Straight down the corridor, through the kitchen, back door is open."

"Maybe some tuna will tempt it. Got any?" she called over her shoulder.

"Er, yeah, I'll have a look. Bound to have." Mike shut the door, locked it, and quietly slipped the chain into place.

He then turned and rushed after Tammy, breathing in her perfume which hung in the air.

Oh, I want more of that.

She'd beaten him to the back garden. And after making a show of banging the kitchen cupboards to search for tuna, he followed her outside.

"No tuna." He sighed exaggeratedly. "Damn."

"Poor little thing." She was staring upwards.

The cat meowed at her. Big blue eyes wide.

"It must be so scared."

"I agree." Mike didn't take his attention off Tammy. He had her here, in his garden, on his property. And it had been so easy.

It was though the universe had put that cat up the tree especially to bring his plan together.

"Do you think you could climb up to get it?" she asked.

"Me? No. When I was a nipper, yes, but not now. A branch would snap, I'd fall to my death." He laughed at the irony. "But look, that branch almost reaches the upstairs window. Perhaps if we open it, the little mite will come in that way, no climbing required."

Tammy turned her attention to the box room window. "That one?"

"Yeah."

"The blind is closed."

He shrugged. "I don't really use it."

"I suppose it's worth a try." She licked her lips then pushed her hair over her shoulders.

It's almost as if she wants me to take her captive.

"Oh yeah, worth a try. Come on, this way." He ushered her back into the house, through the kitchen, and then to the stairs, crossing his fingers she wouldn't notice the lock and chain on the door.

She didn't.

They climbed the stairs, footfalls banging.

Mike stayed close behind, his attention on the globes of her arse.

His excitement was building fast. He was so close. So close to ticking off number one on his bucket list.

"That door there," he said when they reached the top. "Go right in."

"This one?" She gripped the handle.

"Yeah, it's all ready for you."

"Ready?" She frowned, her neatly arched brows coming together. "For me? What do you mean?"

"You'll see."

Chapter Four

"Patrick's wife," Shona said, confusion swimming in her mind. Whatever the hell she'd thought about Earle and Patrick's relationship had just taken a run and jump. Hell, it had dived off the top of a cliff.

"What is she doing here?" Earle stood.

"I guess you'll have to ask her."

"DS, you have a visitor," Darren said. "Fiona Marlborough, wife of DS Patrick Marl—"

"I know who she is." Earle's attention was set on the woman. "Fiona…it's been a while."

"Yes, it has." She clutched her handbag and nibbled on her bottom lip.

"What er…brings you here." Earle slipped his hands into his pockets.

She swallowed and glanced at Shona and then at Darren.

"That's all, thanks, Darren." Shona smiled at him.

"Very good." He turned and walked back through the office.

"Is there somewhere private we can talk?" Fiona asked.

"Yeah, of course, this way." Earle nodded at an empty office beside the coffee machine.

Shona stayed perched against her desk.

"DI," Earle said, pausing and looking over his shoulder.

"You want me there?" she asked.

"Yeah, it's for the best."

"Okay." She set down her drink and followed them into the office.

"Take a seat." Earle dragged out a chair.

"Thanks." Fiona sat and set her bag on the white tabletop.

Shona closed the door. Fiona's attention went to her.

"It's okay," Earle said. "DI Shona Williams is my new partner. Anything you have to say can be said in front of her."

"Are you sure?"

"Absolutely." Earle took a seat opposite her and clasped his big hands on the table.

"You've travelled a fair way," Shona said, positioning herself next to Earle.

"Manchester, took me a couple of hours."

"How is Patrick's recovery going?" Earle asked.

"He is frustrated with everything and everyone."

"Sounds like him."

"He's a rubbish patient." Fiona kind of smiled.

"I'm sure." Earle nodded.

"Won't eat the good stuff, wants treats and cakes. He loves cakes as you know, and…well, he needs to work at recuperation, that's what I keep telling him. Cakes are no good."

Both Shona and Earle were quiet, waiting for Fiona to fill in the silence.

"He asked me to come here," Fiona said. "To see you."

"He did?" Earle raised his eyebrows.

"Yes." She flipped open her handbag and withdrew a plain white envelope.

Shona wriggled on her seat. What on earth was going on? And how had her presumptions been so off the mark? She was usually pretty damn good at reading between the lines.

Patrick is married.

"Fiona, you don't need to do this," Earle said.

"Do what?"

He shook his head, frowned. "This."

"You don't know what I'm doing."

Earle clenched his jaw; a muscle twitched in his cheek.

Does he know what's in there?

"Patrick asked me to give you this." Fiona slid the envelope over the table. "He said you'd know what it meant."

Earle hesitated for a second, then glanced at Shona.

"I suppose there's only one way to find out," she said, nodding at it.

Earle took the envelope. He tore it open then withdrew a single sheet of paper. He didn't hide it from Shona as he unfolded it.

He's back. Watch your back.

Shona kept quiet, there'd be time for questions later.

Earle folded the piece of paper up and slotted it into the envelope again. "Did he have anything else for me?"

"No." She shook her head and redid the clip on her handbag. "But I can tell you something..."

"Go on."

She stood, the handbag now like a shield. "And this is from me, not him."

Earle stood, hands once again in his pockets. "Fiona, I know—"

"I don't think it was an accident."

"What do you mean?" Shona said.

"I know he got in the way, of rival gangs having a tussle, but..." She paused. "I've been married to him for long enough to know when he's not saying something. And this person, this man who shot him, I think he might be from the past. A past he's not proud of, doesn't want to talk about."

"What makes you think that?" Earle asked.

"My husband talks in his sleep." She licked her lips, looked steadily at Earle. "And right now, he's being haunted by a ghost called Bodger...Badger or something like that."

Earle rubbed his temple. "Badger. You're sure?"

"I hear it most nights, when I'm lying next to him."

Earle nodded.

"Does he say anything else?" Shona asked, wondering who the heck Badger was.

"No, but he doesn't have to, it's the way he says it...he's distressed, panicked. I want to wake him up, but they say not to, when someone is having a vivid dream, so I wait until it passes and—"

"It's okay." Earle stepped up and put his hand on her shoulder. "It's okay, Fiona, and thank you for bringing me this letter and for caring for him so well."

"He's my husband. I love him, of course I'm caring for him." Her words were defiant, yet she sniffed and tapped beneath her eyes, as if checking her mascara.

"He's a lucky guy." Earle nodded at the door. "Would you like something to drink before you head back?"

"No, thank you. I'll pop to Greggs, get something from there." She looked at Shona. "I wish you luck here in Ironash."

"Do I need it?"

"It nearly bloody broke me." She tilted her chin. "I'm glad to be out of the place."

Earle pulled open the door. "Would you like me to walk you to your car?"

"No, thank you, I know the way."

"Tell Patrick I appreciate the heads-up."

"I will." She glanced around. "Never thought I'd step foot in this police station again. I hope this really will be the last time."

"Life can be strange," Shona said.

"It can that. I've had things...situations...thrown at me I could never have imagined." She nodded at Earle. "You take care of yourself."

"You, too, Fiona."

She stepped out.

Shona watched her leave the main office and disappear into the lift, then she shut the door and turned to Earle.

He sat at the desk and dropped his head into his hands.

"Well, that was the weirdest start to a Monday morning," she said, "and there's been a few."

He snorted.

She took a seat next to him and opened up the envelope again, pulled out the sheet of paper. "So, now I need to know...who is back?" She ran her fingers over the words.

He was quiet.

"And the DI in me is guessing," she said, "it's someone called Badger."

"Udall Hicks, nickname Badger." Earle ran his hand over his hair. "He's got a grey streak, natural, I think, going over his jet-black hair, hence the name."

"And where has he been?"

"Hospital, prison...I didn't know he was out to tell you the truth."

"And what does it matter that he is?"

"It's complicated."

"Isn't everything." Not least because Fiona had dumped a load more questions in Shona's brain about why she and Patrick had left Ironash.

"Badger was a notorious gang member. Along with his cronies, he roamed the area, they had bikes. Opportunistic thieving was his thing, with a bit of drug dealing, harassment, extortion thrown in. Not into any big buck organised crime, but he'd made a profession of it and wasn't afraid to throw his weight around."

"So he was on the radar."

"Absolutely, and his rap sheet was knocking up with possession of drugs and firearms and ABH. He'd done a few spells at Her Majesty's Pleasure before I came across him."

"You said hospital time. What's that all about?"

Earle sighed.

"Did he get on the wrong side of one of his guns, knives?"

Nothing.

"Hey, mate, if you want me to help you're going to have to tell me the whole story."

"It's not a nice one."

"I've heard plenty of horrors."

"Mmm…"

She rested her hand on his arm. "I'm in your corner, Earle, and if someone is back and you have to watch *your* back, I want to help." Her blood heated just at the thought of someone being out to get her partner. They hadn't worked together long, but their bond had grown quick and was strong. "And for the record, I'm hard to shock."

"It will shock you."

"Try me."

"Can it stay between us, for now? Like I said, it's complicated."

She hesitated. "Fletcher?"

"He knows but…it's sensitive."

"Hey, I'm a woman, sensitive is my middle name, I understand that word perfectly well."

"Yeah, tell that to a bad guy you're kickboxing to the ground."

"Karate, and they deserve it."

"True." He paused. "Two years ago, Patrick and I were on Badger's tail. He'd robbed a cash machine outside Blighty Bingo, along with a couple of accomplices by ramming it with a stolen tractor."

She raised her eyebrows. "Messy."

"Not as messy as the case went."

"Go on."

"We caught him, Badger, on CCTV at the scene, but not the others, though we had a good idea who they were. Trouble was, Badger is good at hiding out in his sett. We didn't hear from him or see him on ANPR for months. The cash machine was fixed up, everything went back to normal."

"And then?"

"And then Patrick and I were at The Hanged Carpenter, watching another suspect on another case, and in strolls Badger, bold as brass, with two of his buddies."

"He'd resurfaced."

"Yeah, and as cocky as ever, though he hadn't noticed the two plain-clothed coppers in the corner."

"Handy."

"It was. So we kept an eye on him, waited to see if we could haul him in on something else and then question him about the cash machine. The more charges the merrier, right?"

Shona had a mind to think she would have just hauled his sorry arse down to the station as soon as she'd seen him but kept that to herself. "So what happened?"

"It all kicked off, you know what it can be like at The Hanged sometimes. Too much Saturday sunshine day drinking by the locals and family feuds, old school, work arguments explode. Badger seemed to be in the middle of it. I watched him smash a bottle on the bar then storm up to a bloke who'd been gobbing off at another fella. So I did what I had to do."

"You tackled him."

"Yeah, to the floor. It just added to the chaos, though. Fights were breaking out all around. I'd lost sight of Patrick, and Badger wasn't being subdued easily."

"He must be a big bloke."

"He is, and he was free and happy with the smashed bottle." Earle undid the top two buttons on his shirt and tugged the material aside. On his dark skin was a raised black scar about three inches long. Stitch dots lined it.

"Shit, that's bad."

"Not really."

"Don't lie. You shouldn't be scarred in the line of duty."

"It happens."

She frowned.

"Anyway, luckily the landlord had called it in and backup was there pretty quickly. The place emptied at the sound of sirens, but still Badger was going for me. I was struggling to hold him back, he got me on my head, too, with the bottle." He rubbed a patch of hair over his left ear. "Patrick finally appeared and helped me get him under control. It wasn't easy…it wasn't gentle."

Shona's heart picked up a notch, and she remembered the word hospital. "What happened to him?"

Earle closed his eyes and squeezed the bridge of his nose.

"Earle?"

"He broke his back."

"What?"

"Fuck, I know…it's bad, isn't it."

"He broke his back?" Shona was shocked. "How the hell did that happen?"

"When I was trying to cuff him. Turns out he's got some kind of bone weakness. A twist with pressure on his spine was enough to break something."

"So he's paralysed?"

"No, not completely, thank God. But he'll always need a stick, or so I was told."

She blew out a breath. "I suppose that's the price he paid for his crimes and resisting arrest."

"That's what the DCI said, and Patrick. I always felt bad about it, but truth was, it could have been me or Patrick. We'd both manhandled him at the end, it was for self-preservation. A shard of broken glass was being waved around like a knife."

"And due force is allowed. You weren't to know he had a calcium deficiency, if that's what it was."

"No, I suppose not. Didn't stop me…us…feeling bad, though."

"As you were being stitched up? Huh, this bloke is a rotten apple, rotten to the core by the sound of it."

"The problem is, rot has a tendency to spread."

"How do you mean?"

"After the court hearing, I found a note in my pocket."

"You *found* it?"

"Yeah, someone with quick fingers had put it there—there was one in Patrick's, too."

"What did it say?"

"Your judgement day will arrive. Guess who will be judge!"

"Forensics?"

"It was clean, no prints. But we both knew it was from Badger."

"Threatening a police officer is a serious offence."

"If it can be proven."

"True."

"Trouble was, his complaints about rough handling had been quashed by the court."

"Which is fair enough, you'd only used due force."

"We knew that, DCI Fletcher knew that, but still it was an embarrassment for Ironash Police, so it was kept as quiet as possible, a need-to-know basis. And definitely out of the papers. Fletcher has a way of handling things."

"Another reason for Badger to be pissed off. He'd have wanted to shout loud about what had happened."

"Which he couldn't do from custody."

"And now he has a bee in his bonnet."

"A need for revenge, a need to seek his own justice. And by the sounds of it, he's already had a good go at Patrick. Which means he wants a piece of me, too."

"Which he won't get." Shona tapped the envelope. "Patrick and Fiona have given you a warning. Now you know, *we* know, we can keep our eyes and ears peeled." She paused. "But why would Fiona make the trip? Why not just call or post it?"

He shrugged. "I'm guessing to make sure I was here."

"What do you mean?"

"Settled, not about to transfer to Manchester."

That surprised Shona. "Would you want to?"

He was quiet for a heartbeat then, "Absolutely not."

Chapter Five

Mike rammed Tammy between the shoulder blades, hurtling her into the spare room.

She gasped and stumbled, her handbag slipping from her shoulder to the crook of her arm.

Two big strides, and he was in the room with her, back-kicking the door closed with a slam.

"What are you doing?" She spun to face him, a long strand of hair catching in the corner of her mouth.

"Making you mine." He loomed over her, staring into her eyes.

Even through the gloom he could see her pupils were wide, and all the whites were visible around her irises. Her brow was creased and her lips parted.

"Let me go." She shoved at him.

He grinned. She was as weak as a gnat—this was going to be easy.

"I mean it, let me go. I'll scream." This time she tried to circumnavigate him.

Mike blocked her way. "I want a woman," he said. "You will do nicely."

Her bottom lip was trembling, her eyes misting. "You could have asked for a date. That would be the normal thing to do." She'd tried to inject some strength into her voice, but Mike heard the underlying fear.

A rush of blood went to his groin.

"And would you have said yes?" he asked.

She hesitated.

He laughed and gripped her shoulders, pushed her towards the bed and being sure to dig his fingers in hard. "My point exactly, and between you and me, I don't have time to mess around with dates."

"Mike! Let me go, I mean it, I'll scream, I…"

He grabbed the ball gag and held it between them. "You can try." Quick as a flash, and glad he'd practised, he thrust the black ball into her mouth. Her jaw stretched prettily, and her eyes grew even wider.

"Mmmm...." She twisted her head, this way and that, trying to escape him.

He was pleased by the lack of noise she could make.

Suddenly, a pain slashed over his right cheek.

"Ah, bitch."

She'd scraped her talon-like nails down his skin, sensitive and thin from months of being systematically poisoned by chemo. He knew she'd cut deep.

He hurled her to the bed, warm liquid running to his jawline.

She landed with a whump but righted herself. Her hands went to the strap holding the ball gag in place.

"Oh no you don't." He was on top of her, pinning her with his body. She was so delicate and soft beneath him that memories of *her* came rushing back, heightening his excitement. "You might as well just accept what's happening." He dragged her hands over her head, then secured her wrists in the cuffs. "Because it *is* happening. You are mine."

A fat drip of ruby-red blood landed on her chin.

He felt his cheek. It was wet with the warm stuff. "And you'll pay for that."

Happy she was secure, he stood and dragged off his t-shirt. He balled the material and pressed it over the claw marks stretching down his face.

"Mmm...mmm..." She battled against the cuffs, her shoulders, torso, and hips flicking this way and that. Her breasts heaved and jostled, and her hair fanned out on the pillow like some kind of damn Disney princess.

"There's no point in all that," he said. "There's no escape, you're mine, and you will be for a few months, not years, just months, if that snippet of information helps." He stroked his crooked index finger over her chin, smearing the drip of his own blood. "And I'm going to have a wonderful time with you." He chuckled, a delicious mix of anticipation and desire winging around his body. "Perhaps you'll even enjoy it."

She snapped her head away from his touch and kicked her heels, making the whole bed rattle against the wall.

Not that it mattered.

"You're well and truly my prisoner," he said, straightening. "And once I've seen to this." He pointed to his cheek. "I'll be back."

"Mmm..."

"What was that? No? Let me go? Tough, you don't get a say in it. You are my gift to myself."

Mike left the room, a warm satisfied glow settling in his stomach that he knew would just intensify as the day went on.

And how simple it had been.

Two hours later, and feeling on top of the world, Mike flicked the nets to peer out of the window.

His buoyant mood deflated like a popped balloon.

"Fuck it."

Tammy's car was still parked up. Just sat there, like a damn Belisha beacon announcing she wasn't about to drive away in it. Bloody thing might as well have a sign on it saying that she was harnessed naked to a bed in his house.

I have to get rid of it.

He paced across the living room, running his fingers through his hair, then grabbing his jumper and slipping it on. He'd got the chills now, bloody car.

His gaze landed on her bag which he'd slung onto the armchair.

With shaking hands, he rooted through it. He drew out her phone.

"Fuck." He turned it off and removed the SIM card which he dropped into a glass containing the last dregs of whisky. He found her keys in a side pocket beside the tassels. "Gotcha." He threw them into the air and caught them with a snap of his wrist.

He rushed from the room, paused with his hand on the newel, and looked up the stairs.

All was quiet, and he knew full well she couldn't go anywhere. If Tammy could get out of those cuffs, she definitely would have in order to escape what he'd just done to her.

She was going nowhere.

After ramming his feet into his boots, he grabbed a lightweight jacket. Hands on the chain, he stopped and stared at his fingers.

Phew, that was close.

He ran into the kitchen and pulled out a pair of the thin latex gloves he'd had to wear if handling his long-line, to stop it getting infected. They would do perfectly.

After putting them on, he let himself out of the front door then rammed his hands into his pockets. He paused. The street was deserted except for a dog walker at the far end, likely heading to the towpath.

He dashed to the car. It was risky, he knew that, but it really would only take a moment to get in and drive away.

If he could remember how to drive a manual, that was.

He unlocked it, slid into the driver's seat, then started the engine. Without waiting, he accelerated forward.

He lurched. The engine died.

"Bugger."

He'd stalled the ruddy thing.

A glance at Mrs Robin's house showed empty windows, meaning she was probably in her back garden. Good. Only the dumb gnomes to see him disposing of evidence, and they were mute.

He started the car again, let the clutch up slowly, and after only one pitch forward, drove to the end of the street.

He indicated left, heart racing, and turned onto the main road out of the estate. He knew exactly where to go. It was where he always went when he needed to get rid of something.

Ealing Woods.

Heart hammering, he slunk down in the seat, wishing he could be an invisible driver. What if someone Tammy knew spotted it wasn't her driving her car? What if CCTV picked him up on camera? He hated the fact Big Brother was always watching. No damn privacy these days.

He passed the rubbish truck, which was crawling along, the blokes chucking black bags into the back, then had to pause to wait for the ice-cream van to take a left.

"Fucking noisy thing," he muttered as the tinny tune rattled around the inside of Tammy's car. "Why can't the man just have a heart attack or something." He clicked his tongue on the top of his mouth. "Better still, cancer, that would get rid of him, save me having to listen to that moronic tune every day for the rest of my life."

He frowned, and, still muttering, overtook the ice-cream van, pressing a little harder on the accelerator when he read the stupid 'kill your speed, not a child' sign on the back.

Within a few minutes he was on Six Mile Lane. The long road was bordered with arable fields. The one to his right was high with wheat crop swaying in the slight breeze. Soon it would be harvested, mowed down, just the stubble left.

The treeline of Ealing Woods rose in the distance. Dark and tall, the pine trees' sharp points pricking the blue sky.

Mike's heart rate settled.

He'd dump the car then walk back, it would only take an hour or so. Six Mile Lane wasn't actually six miles, it was only four. Bloody daft name for it really.

A police car was heading towards him, on the opposite side of the road. No flashing lights or siren, but still, Mike tightened his grip on the steering wheel, and a shot of adrenaline burst into his bloodstream.

"Keep calm, Mikey-boy."

There was no reason for them to stop him, or be suspicious. No way could they see the scratches on his face from this distance. No, he was just a bloke driving his car. Perfectly innocent. Perfectly normal.

The police car went past. There was only one occupant. A uniformed female.

"Huh." He shook his head. "If she had stopped me, well...I could have had some more fun." He chuckled and unflexed his fingers.

A few more minutes down the road he turned right. Here, just after the Downing Farm lay-by, the lane was darkened by the canopy of trees which met overhead, creating a vivid green tunnel.

There were no other cars. All was quiet, just the way he'd hoped.

One hundred yards farther, he took an overgrown track leading west. He'd used it before, back then, to find a place to dig a shallow grave.

Memories flooded his mind as Tammy's car creaked over a hole then tipped into a dip. But what did it matter if the suspension complained, or in fact broke? She'd never use this car again...or any car for that matter.

He nibbled his bottom lip, tugging at a bit of skin with his teeth. His lips had been cracked and dry from the first day of the damn chemo. How long would he let her live? A few days, a week, a month? He didn't know at this point but he guessed it would be a juggling act of how easy she was to keep, how much pleasure he could take from her before he got deathly sick, and how he intended to dispose of her. Perhaps he'd just leave her tied to the bed when he took himself off to the hospice. Might be comforting to know he wasn't the only one dying over those few days.

He glanced left and right at the mulched woodland floor. Here it was uneven, and anthills were dotted randomly between the trees. Not easy to walk on but easy enough to dig. The perfect combination for body burying as he'd found out.

But a car?

That wasn't going to be so easy.

A small clearing in the trees led to a large dank ditch. The water was stagnant, dark bugs swarmed, and several lichen-dotted branches touched fingers over it.

"That'll have to do."

He drove up to it, bouncing on the seat and almost whacking his head when the car pitched into a dip.

Grunting, he came to a halt, the front bumper only inches from the slope leading to the water. He didn't apply the handbrake.

He shut the engine down and got out. He removed the keys and pocketed them—no point in risking fingerprints.

Then he went around to the back of the car and set his palms on the boot. He gave it a heave, grimaced when it barely moved and inch, then found a firmer footing and pushed again.

This time it moved, and the more it moved, the quicker it went. Soon it was rolling into the water. Quietly, softly, no drama, no big splash. Just a gentle slip into the dark mouth.

He straightened and placed his hands on his hips. If the universe was truly on his side it would be completely submerged. But of course, that didn't happen. It came to a stop just past the driver's door, the back end sticking up rudely.

He tutted and frowned. It would have been ideal for it to disappear completely, but realistically, that was never going to happen. But with a bit of luck it wouldn't be found for a few weeks, and then with no evidence of him in it, the car would still be a dead end to Tammy's disappearance.

He laughed at that. Dead End. It really was going to be a dead end, for all of them.

After a last look around, and wondering if he could remember exactly where *she* was, he headed back along the track he'd just driven down. Her body would be gone by now, he was sure of it. Unless she'd become like the body in the bog and was preserved. What was that old Neanderthal called? Pete or something because he'd been found in peat.

Mike strode forward, tugging off his latex gloves in case he came across anyone. But he doubted it. This was a quiet place, not frequented by dog walkers due to its lack of useable paths.

He glanced at his watch. He'd get his head down and quicken his pace, return to Tammy. Maybe there'd be time for more fun before dinner. It had been a long while since he'd had access to a woman's body, might as well make the most of it.

He walked along the tunnel of trees. A squirrel ran out in front of him then scampered up a trunk. A pair of jays squawked their displeasure of him being there.

"Yeah," he huffed. "You should be scared. I'm not a nice person, and now, I have no reason to pretend to be." The date of his deathday had wiped his need to appear a decent human being, even if all along Mike had known he was anything but. He had a healthy dose of monster running through his veins. An evil gene in his DNA that he was sure had come from his nan. And, it seemed, he also had a total absence of conscience.

"Yeah, what do I care." He smiled, enjoying the moment of self-acceptance and being true to his desires for once.

It was then he saw it, the familiar yellow front of the ice-cream van.

It was parked up in Downing Farm lay-by, the only vehicle there, and, unbelievably, with the damn engine running, black smoke chugging from the exhaust. Mike could even smell it.

"What the fuck." He approached at a swift pace.

The driver was sitting in the front, head back, eyes closed, catching flies. His double chins sat heavily on his throat, and his white t-shirt had a blob of something red on it—could be ketchup, could be strawberry sauce.

When Mike reached the van, he hammered on the driver's window. "Hey, you."

The man started, his eyes wide, his mouth opening and closing like a fish out of water. He twisted this way and that, pressed his hand to his chest, and finally focused on Mike. He wound down the window a few inches. "What?"

"Why've you got your engine running? Polluting the woods, that's what you're doing."

"It's none of your business." He frowned, his bald head seeming to melt into his brow.

"It is my business, I'm breathing this air. Trying to kill me, are you?" Mike jabbed his finger in the direction of the exhaust.

The van driver sighed. "If you must know, it's keeping the ice cream solid. Hot day, it is, don't want it to melt."

"Would do us all a favour if it did."

"What do you mean by that?"

"You. This." Mike shook his head as his hate for the ice-cream van filled his veins and quickened his heart rate. It was like red-hot treacle flowing through him, heating his cheeks, making his scalp itch. "You're a menace to society."

The man shook his head. "Piss off, will you, I'm taking my break."

"What we all need is a break from you. Peaceful place, Ironash, then you go around with your stupid music and your polluting van, getting all the kids sugared up and—"

"You're a bloody loony, knob off."

The red-hot treacle feeling intensified. Hate flicked to rage. Mike's knees shook a little as if they were ready to spring into action. He balled his fists, and his shoulders tensed. There was only one thing to do, for himself and his fellow citizens—get rid of this man.

Plus, he'd seen Mike now, hadn't he. Coming back from the woods. Woods where he'd just dumped the car of a soon-to-be-reported-missing woman.

Mike put his gloves back on, then yanked the handle of the ice-cream van door. To his surprise, it opened.

"Hey. What are you doing?" the fat driver said.

"What's your name?"

"Barry, not that it's any of your business."

"Well, Barry, I'm going to show you just how much your mind-numbing music and filthy van have pissed me off over the years."

"Fuck off." He lurched for the door, scrabbling with podgy fingers, and tried to close it.

But Mike was fast, and he wrenched it out of reach then grabbed Barry's right upper arm and dragged him from the vehicle.

He half fell, half stumbled out, landing on the ground with a thud. In an instant he was throwing a meaty-fisted punch Mike's way.

But Mike wasn't about to take a hit, so he side-stepped then landed a hard one on Barry's jaw.

A string of spittle flew from his mouth and he thumped up against the van, his shoulder taking the impact. He groaned and turned around. "Why are you doing this?"

"*Porque eu posso, idiota.*"

"What?" His eyes flashed, real fear in them.

"I said...because I can, idiot." Mike puffed up his chest, revelling in the returning sense of power after having been poisoned with the chemo until he was sick and weak and barely able to get out of bed. Now he was back, a month of eating, a woman, and he was as good as he was ever going to be.

"Please, let me go. The float is in the back."

"I don't want money."

"There's about fifty quid. Take it." Barry slipped to the left, going for the driver's seat again.

Mike slammed the door shut, as hard as he could.

Too bad Barry's hand was in the way.

He yelled and clutched his squashed piggy fingers. Two of the nails had been crushed, and blobs of blood were rising on the ends.

"You bastard."

"That's nothing, you son of a bitch." Mike snatched hold of his other hand, held it firm against the van's doorframe, then slammed the door again.

He did it so fast Barry barely even tried to resist.

He let out another yelp of pain, his hands shaking as he raised them to study the ribbons of skin hanging off.

Mike took the opportunity to land one on his nose. His fist connected with a satisfying bone crunch.

"Argh!" Barry wailed.

"You need to shut up." Mike grabbed the back of Barry's t-shirt and hauled him around the van, to the grassy bank near the trees. It wouldn't do to have someone drive past and spoil his fun.

"Let me go, please. I have a wife, kids…" Barry stumbled, blood running from his nose and into his mouth.

"And I'm sure they'll miss you."

"Miss me? What are you going to—?"

Mike punched him in the guts, throwing all of his weight behind the hit the way he used to when in the ring.

Barry doubled over, breath huffing from his lungs along with an agonised groan.

Mike was enjoying himself, the most he had since…well, since Tammy earlier in the afternoon. Yeah, it was proving to be a particularly good day, all things considered.

He hit out again and again. Reminding himself of how he'd been so good at rib shots, kidney shots, below-the-belt shots. His skin heated; a trickle of sweat ran from his temple to his cheek. He got the familiar buzz of controlling a fight, being the one to overpower. It was a break not to think of the Big C's dominating force.

Barry was shrinking, lowering to the ground, curling over himself as though trying to reduce his surface area.

That made Mike laugh. Did he really think anything would save him now? Barry was going to meet his maker. Mike hoped he'd been a good boy and not the lazy shitbag he gave the impression of being.

Mike threw in a few kicks. Striking Barry on the head, his hard boots landing in his eye sockets, his ears and his jaw. A tooth flew onto the ground, then another.

Mike upped the tempo and the power. Barry's skull was caving in, taking the beating full force.

He'd stopped crying out and was no longer trying to escape. Now he lay there like a pathetic little kid, not even trying to avoid the boot, the beating.

"That all you got?" Mike shouted, dislocating Barry's jaw with a well-aimed strike. "After annoying me for years, that's all the fight back I'm going to get. A big guy like you."

Mike was breathless and hot. His blood winged through his veins, spreading triumph to every cell.

Eventually he stopped and stared down at Barry's listless, bloody body.

Is he breathing?

Mike squatted next to him, elbows on his thighs, hands dangling, and watched his chest.

Nothing.

He stared some more, the familiar thrill of having killed in the woods sparking a fire of excitement inside his belly. "Not so loud now, are you, twat?"

And then suddenly a stone was flying his way. It connected with the side of his head, just above his ear, sending a sharp, violent pain shooting through his head.

Mike reeled backwards, the force of it toppling him. He almost landed on his arse but rectified himself just in time.

"You bastard." He jumped to his feet, seized the stone from Barry's hand, and brought it down on his face.

The second hard connection, on his forehead, was the one that did it. The light snapped off in Barry's eyes.

"Dead now, aren't you." Mike kept on pounding his face, breaking every bone, mashing every bit of flesh with the stone. On and on he went, knowing blood was flying around, that he was making one hell of a mess. But he didn't care, it was like being a bull on a mission to get that red rag. He kept on going, using up all of the hate in his system on Barry's ugly mangled face.

Chapter Six

"Ma'am, I've got one for you," Darren said.

"Go on." Shona stood. She'd be heading out the door in the next minute. She knew Darren well enough to hear 'that' tone in his voice—the one that meant someone had come to a bad end and it was her and Earle's job to find out the who, why, and what of the situation.

Earle copied her and stood, slipping his phone and keys into his pocket.

"A farmer has made a rather grim discovery in the lay-by near his wheat field."

"Go on."

"An ice-cream van."

"An ice-cream van?" She pulled a face at Earle. "How is that grim?"

Earle shrugged.

"Yeah," Darren went on, "there's no driver but rather a lot of blood next to it. Definitely needs investigating."

"You're not wrong there. Where is it?"

"Just off Six Mile Lane."

Shona suppressed a shudder. Once upon a time she'd been dumped naked on Six Mile Lane with her memory wiped. But she'd moved on from that now, it was the only way to go forward with her life.

"There's a small lane, leading to Ealing Woods," Darren continued. "Seemed the ice-cream man often stopped there for a break, in the lay-by, the farmer said. Didn't get hassled by kids, I suppose."

She headed for the stairs. "We're on our way. Thanks."

"Shall I send SOCO?"

"We'll check it out first, make sure it's not strawberry sauce and the ice-cream man is just having a wee in the woods."

"Very good, ma'am."

"Strawberry sauce?" Earle said as they went down the stairs.

"Seems a farmer has found a suspicious red fluid next to an ice-cream van parked up near Ealing Woods."

"Ealing Woods. Last time we went there it was on the Umbridge case."

"Uh, don't remind me, that poor young man who'd had his hand chopped off and bled to death. Hard to believe a girl did that to him."

"A very disturbed girl, one out for vengeance."

His last word hung in the air as they walked to his car. He was thinking of Badger.

"We could tell Fletcher, get some uniform outside your house," she suggested.

"What? Just in case a bloke from an old case appears? If we all felt like that, uniform wouldn't do anything else." He unlocked his car, and it flashed awake.

Shona climbed into the passenger seat. They always used Earle's car. He could barely fit inside her VW Beetle. "I think it's a bit different when Badger has already had a pop at your ex partner and—"

"We don't even know if Badger is back in town." Earle started the four-by-four. "Let alone out for vengeance against me."

Shona fastened her seat belt and held in her opinion. Badger was out of jail, and Ironash was his hometown. Chances of him being back here, or heading back, were pretty high. And if he was the scumbag she believed him to be, and it was him who'd got a few hits on Patrick, then Earle had a right to some kind of protection.

Earle drove away. "I'm not in the habit of getting spooked, and I'm not going to start now."

"Okay, fair enough. But we should consider telling Fletcher about the situation. It's not new news to him about Badger being injured during arrest and his complaints about manhandling being quashed."

"No, it's not. But I'd rather not dig it up, unless something happens."

"Like *you* getting shot?" The words had spilled from her lips quicker than she'd intended.

"Cheers for that." He tutted.

"I'm sorry, I...let's just make a deal. The first whiff of Badger being around, then we tell Fletcher. If he's armed and not afraid to point the barrel of a gun at a police officer, then we can't take any chances."

"Fair enough, but Patrick probably got it wrong and Badger wasn't involved at all in his shooting. You know how confusing these situations can be, everything happens so fast."

"Is Patrick wrong often?" She set her attention on Earle.

He glanced at her. "What do you think?"

"I think he's not."

They drove out of Ironash in silence. Shona suddenly felt very protective of Earle and was eyeballing each car they passed. What if someone really did have him in their sights? What if something happened to him?

She hugged her arms around herself. What-ifs did no good, she'd learnt that over the years. What counted was action.

Earle slowed when they reached the lane at the end of the wheat field. As they turned into it, she removed her sunglasses. The road was shaded by trees which gave it a green-hued, magical appearance.

"There's the ice-cream van." Earle nodded ahead.

A police car was parked up behind it.

"I hope there's been no scene contamination," she said, shaking her head.

"And it will be a crime scene. If a uniform is hanging about, chances of the driver having spilt strawberry sauce and gone for a piss are slim to none."

"Yep."

Earle pulled up.

The uniform got out of his car and strolled over.

Shona and Earle walked to meet him.

"Hi, Damon, how are you?" Shona said.

"Had better days." The young PC shook his head. "Darren told me to swing in here as I was passing."

"What have you found?"

"Not much because it's a scene." He pointed at the van. "Blood and shit all over the ground there."

"Body?"

"No, nothing. I haven't got any protectives so I had a quick scout around, called out, but I didn't want to mess anything up. I knew you were only a few minutes away."

"Good man. Can you start a log, please." Shona retrieved a white protective from Earls' car boot and slipped into it, then added booties and gloves.

Earle did the same.

"Here." Damon handed over a pen and file.

Shona took it, signed her name, and added the time. She gave it to Earle. "Are SOCO on the way?"

"Not yet, I was waiting for you, ma'am."

She nodded and walked to the van. Straight away she spotted blood on the door, then as she went around to the other side, where the serving window was, she saw the mess. "Jesus," she muttered. "Not just blood, appears to be bone and teeth, too. There's been a right old fight here."

"Shit." Earle stood at her side and gestured into the woods. "Dogs?"

"Good idea. And SOCO."

"I'll get Damon on it." He stepped away.

"Why would anyone kill an ice-cream man?" She looked from the bloody grass bank to the van. It was bright yellow with cartoon characters drawn on the side. The serving window, currently slid shut, was full of sun-faded images of ice lollies and ice creams along with the prices.

The window at the front, on the passenger door, caught her attention. On it was written—in red— *a vingança é doce*.

What did it mean? What language was it?

She pulled out her phone and typed it into a translation app. Language recognised, Portuguese. *Revenge is sweet.*

"Seems like someone had a beef with the ice-cream man," she said as Earle joined her again.

He read the screen on her phone and frowned.

"That's what it says, on that window." She pointed. "In Portuguese."

"Bloody hell." He stared at it. "Is that written in blood?"

"I'm guessing so." She carefully stepped up to the van. "We should take a nose inside."

"Dogs are on the way," Damon called.

"Good." Shona gestured to the road. "Can we block this off? I don't want anyone coming and going from the scene."

"Yes, ma'am."

"Just when I thought Ironash had had its full quota of murders for one year." Earle scratched his head.

"We don't know this is a murder," Shona said, climbing into the cab of the van.

"Yet…" Earle followed her, though he really didn't appear comfortable stooped almost double.

"Licence here." Shona pointed to a small laminated card with a photograph of a chubby bald bloke on it. "A Barry White."

"Barry White. You have to be kidding me."

"Nope." Shona climbed into the back. It smelled sickly sweet. The floor was littered with ice creams and lollies. They were imploding as they melted, and some seeped white, blue, green, and brown goo from their wrappers.

"Money is still here," she said, nodding at a float on the side.

"Hmm." Earle moved in next to her in a strange hunched shuffle. "Wasn't a robbery on top of revenge then."

"Apparently not."

"Any idea why Portuguese?"

"Your guess is as good as mine." She gripped the handle of the large freezer which took up one whole side of the van.

"Why do you think the ice creams have been tossed out?" Earle pulled a face.

"Only one way to find out." Shona gritted her teeth, then opened the lid of the freezer.

"Oh fuck," Earle said.

Shona blew out a breath and lifted the lid fully. Staring up at her was, presumably, Barry White. Though he was more red than white. His face gave the impression that it had had a run-in with a combine harvester. His eyes were ballooned and purple, the lids almost shut. His cheeks were a mess, the skin split and gaping. And his mouth, it was clear he'd taken a boot there a few times—his teeth were either gone or hanging out, and his tongue had a snake-like split in the end.

Shona checked for a pulse. "Dead."

"No shit, Sherlock," Earle muttered.

"Damn it." She tutted. "Poor bugger."

Earle pointed to Barry's hand. "I'd say he had a bit of a fight back, his hands are a mess."

"Too messy for a fight. They appear crushed, like the ends of the fingers have been trapped in a door."

"Yeah, you're right. I noticed blood on the driver's door."

"Me, too."

She shut the lid. "Let's get out of here, there's nothing we can do for him."

They shuffled out. "It's a bit of a squeeze," Earle said.

"Yes, and Barry's not a small bloke from what I can tell. Can't have been easy working conditions."

"Or easy to lift him into the freezer."

"So we're searching for a strong fella as the culprit." She stepped down onto the ground and placed her hands on her hips. "Someone strong enough to overpower him, beat him up outside, and then lift him into the van. Not easy, certainly I couldn't lift him."

"But I could." Earle dropped to his haunches and examined the ground. "It's a bit damp, there might be boot prints."

"You're right, lets move away so we don't disturb it."

They headed to the front of the van, Shona studying the area. It was certainly a strange case, right from the get-go.

"Shall we..." Earle nodded into the woods.

"No harm in that." She called to Damon. "We're heading into the trees."

"Right you are, ma'am. SOCO are only ten minutes away."

"Great."

They changed their booties and gloves. Within ten feet of being in the treeline, the gloom closed in. The trunks were close together, and there were no real pathways to search for footprints.

They stuck together, went farther, not really knowing what they were searching for but hoping something would stand out.

"Do you think you can get to the road from here?" Shona asked.

"Probably, if you don't mind getting a few scratches along the way." Earle pushed a spiked branch away from his face. "I'd say it would take about ten, fifteen minutes."

"So maybe he parked on Six Mile Lane then walked to the scene?" She was thinking out loud.

"Or next to the ice-cream van."

"Yes, that's more likely." But why did she have a feeling the killer was on foot? It was like a gut tightening, an instinct. She didn't know why it was there but she wouldn't ignore it, even if she pushed it aside for a while.

Earle stopped. "I don't think there's any point going farther. The dogs will do a sweep of the area."

"Yes, you're right." She paused. "What was that?" She spun to the right at the sound of another crack, like a twig snapping.

Earle frowned and stared in the same direction. "I don't know," he whispered. "But I heard it, too."

"Is there someone there?" she called

She held still, not wanting to make any sound.

Through the shadows there appeared to be nothing but tree trunks and dips and rises in the ground where the ants had stacked up their homes. It was impossible to see more than twenty or thirty metres before darkness took over.

"Shall we take a look?" Earle asked.

Shona's heart rate picked up. "Yes, we should."

They inched forward, trying to keep noise to a minimum. She bent a thin branch from her line of view, then spotted a flash of movement, about shoulder height.

"Yes, straight ahead." She sped up. "I saw something."

Earle pressed on, his long legs covering the ground.

"Be careful," she said, suddenly feeling vulnerable in this alien territory. It was hard to keep footing, hard to move with any speed.

Earle kept on going, and because he was ahead of her she had to stop branches twanging back and swiping over her cheeks. Her belly clenched; her reflexes had to be quick.

But could they catch the individual lurking in the woods?

After several minutes, the trees thinned, and sunlight flooded the pine needles carpeting the ground. A patch of fat-headed mushrooms squeezed up through the mulch.

Earle halted at a fence that separated the woods from Six Mile Lane. He set his hands on it and leaned forward, breathing hard and looking left and right along the road. "I was sure I heard something."

"I was sure I saw something."

"But there's nothing here, the road is deserted."

It was true. Left and right, for as far as the eye could see on the ruler-straight road, there were no cars. If someone had been only a minute ahead of them, they hadn't got away. "It's a good job dogs are going to sniff out the area."

"Yeah." Earle nodded and scanned the shadows they'd just come through.

"The culprit could be lying low." Shona peered into every dip and at every trunk, scanning for the shape of a body or a face.

Nothing.

"The culprit," Earle repeated.

"Mmm…"

"Or," he said.

"Or?" She frowned at him.

He swallowed. "Badger. What if it's him? Following me."

Chapter Seven

Mike let himself into his house and as usual chained and locked the front door. He was out of breath—he'd rushed from the scene, head down, hands shoved into his pockets, and not slowed until now.

Luckily, the road had been quiet—all he'd seen was the tractor going into the wheat field, other than that, just the number twenty-eight bus and a handful of cars.

He leaned back against the door and held out his hands. They were bloody and the knuckles swollen, not that he minded. It was like the old days when he'd been fighting. He turned them over, examining the ruby splatters on each side. He'd have to ice them, get the puffiness down. It wouldn't do to have anyone ask him about them.

"Got what you deserved, didn't you, fat boy," he muttered, thinking of the ice-cream man's face when he'd shut the lid of the freezer. It hadn't been easy to get him in there, he'd had to throw all of the stupid ice creams out of it, but it had seemed such a fitting end he couldn't resist.

He chuckled and tugged off his t-shirt. It would likely be covered in ice-cream man's DNA, same with his boots. They all needed a clean, and he needed a shower.

After pulling the latex gloves from his pocket and shoving them in the bin, inside a crisp packet for extra hiding, he flicked the kettle on and whacked a frozen cottage pie into the oven.

Mike went up the stairs.

It had been inspired to add the note on the van window in the victim's blood. *A vingança é doce.* He'd read enough books, seen enough BBC dramas to know that all killers had a calling card. Well, that was his. He hadn't managed anything the first time, hadn't thought back then, in the woods, but now he had an MO. Perhaps he'd even go down in history as the Cryptic Killer or the Portuguese Pest. Yeah, that was good, plus it would throw them off the scent. They'd be hunting for a foreigner now, not someone who didn't even own a passport.

On the landing, he hovered outside *her* room, listening.

All was quiet.

Too quiet.

His heart seemed to skip a beat then double up on the next one, making a weird lolloping sensation in his chest.

"Shit." He gritted his teeth. Had she managed to get away? He bloody hoped not, that would spoil his end-of-days fun.

He opened the door to the darkened room. A wash of relief came over him.

She was still laid on the bed, arms locked above her head, blindfold in place, if a little askew. She'd managed to drag the duvet over her legs and almost up to her waist, but her voluptuous breasts were bare and hung heavy to either side.

"Mmmm...mm...mm...mm," she mumbled as she faced his direction.

"What was that, let you go? Why would I do that?" He released the strap holding her gag in place.

She licked her lips, her tongue poking out shakily. "I...I won't tell anyone what you did, I promise. Let's just forget this ever happened."

"You expect me to believe that?"

"It's a promise. I believe in promises."

"Well, I don't, and I know full well, the minute you step out of this door you'll be running to the bloody coppers."

"I won't, I swear. My mother will be so worried, I see her every day, please..." She sobbed, her bottom lip quivering.

It was quite sweet really.

"Mike, I just want to go home...I know you're not a bad man really, we can—"

"Shut up, I don't want to listen to your whining." He frowned.

"But you can't keep me here."

"I can."

She was quiet for a moment, then, "I need to pee."

"What?" Fuck. He hadn't thought of that.

"And I'm thirsty, please let me have a drink of water." She raised her head from the pillow. "I need a drink."

Mike shoved his hand down his trousers and adjusted himself. She really was very pretty, and her tits were lush. Actually, her mouth was, too.

"I'll take you to the toilet and get you a drink, after..."

"After what?" There was a shake in her voice.

He loved that, too. "After I've done what I brought you here for. After I've taken what I want."

Half an hour later, and Mike wandered into his back garden to harvest some runner beans to go with his cottage pie. He was hungry, and he relished the sensation after months of nausea. It was still a treat to decide what he fancied to eat and know he'd still want it when it was cooked, and better still, keep it down.

A cloud crossed over the sun, bringing the garden into shade, but only for a few seconds, and by the time he'd reached his vegetable patch, the heat was basting his shoulders again.

Satisfaction felt so good.

Why did I wait so long to get myself a woman?

He picked a handful of runner beans then stooped to check the lettuce. He ran his fingers over the tender lime-green leaves.

It was then he spotted it.

Cat poo.

"Fucking thing." He gripped the lettuce and dragged it from the earth. Soil sprinkled in its wake. "How can I eat this now?"

It was the annoying fluffy cat from the house behind. It had to be, no one else had one, they were all dog lovers. And the bloody thing had taken, lately, to using his beloved vegetable patch as a toilet.

He stomped up to the six-foot fence that separated the two gardens and lobbed the lettuce over it. An arc of dusty mud followed.

"Hey!"

Mike paused for a second, not expecting to have had a reaction from his leafy missile.

"What the fuck are you doing?" Fingertips appeared over the fence, then the top of a head and eyeballs. "I don't want your spring greens."

Mike folded his arms, hiding his bruised knuckles. "Your cat."

"What about it?"

"Comes in my garden all the time. Up the tree, shitting in my veg."

"So what do you expect me to do about it?" the man snapped.

"Stop it."

"How? It's a cat, they go where they want."

"I don't want it in my garden."

"Tough."

"Keep it in the house."

"It's not a bloody house cat, and I don't want to have to clean out a litter tray."

"It's using my garden as a litter tray."

"So put egg shells down, or lemon juice or something." He cackled. "But I'll tell you what…"

"What?"

"I'll have a word, tell her not to do it anymore." He laughed harder. "That should do it."

Mike bristled. "I'll kill the fucking cat."

A pause, then, "What?"

"I'll kill it. Next time I see it in my garden, I'll strangle her stupid fluffy neck, throttle it."

"You can't do that to Muffy. I'll have the RSPCA on you."

"How will you know it's me?"

"Because…because you just said you were going to do it." There was a note of alarm in his voice now.

"So keep it...what's your name?"

"Wayne."

"Keep it, Wayne, out of my garden."

Wayne was quiet for a moment, then, "What happened to your face?"

Mike touched his cheek, where Tammy had clawed him. "That was your damn cat, too. Got stuck up my tree, I had to get it down. Ungrateful bitch scratched me."

"So don't touch her. Muffy knows a bad sort when she sees one, obviously." Wayne's eyes, head, and fingertips disappeared. "Twat," he muttered from the other side of the fence.

Mike spread his fingers wide then clenched them into fists. He stared at the fence where Wayne had just been. His heart was clattering up against his ribs, and a familiar heat wended its way over his scalp, down his neck and spine to his belly.

His abdomen tensed as the anger bloomed. It had started off small, like a seed, but now had grown into the size of a football, pushing up, pressing on his insides. It would need to be deflated, released.

And there was only one way to do that.

Wayne would have to meet the Portuguese Pest.

When darkness fell, Mike ensured *she* was tied up securely with ball gag in place then put on black jeans, a black t-shirt, and a pair of latex gloves.

He checked the chain on the front door, put the TV on so it gave the impression he was home, then slipped into the back garden. There was a full moon, and the tree, vegetable patch, and fence were lit with a silvery glow.

Quickly, he dragged a patio chair to the fence and stood on it.

Wayne's house was in darkness except for one upstairs window.

Good. Wayne the Pain was getting ready for bed, or better still, he was in bed. That would make it easier. Give Mike the element of true surprise. He liked the idea of that.

Mike glanced left and right, then hopped over the fence. He landed on the lawn with a soft whump. For a moment he stayed crouched, stealth-like, reminding himself of a movie star in a big adventure role—Tom Cruise, Bruce Willis, Harrison Ford. Grinning and wishing he'd camo'd up his face for effect, he slunk to Wayne's back door. He didn't even try it, he knew it would be locked. But that wouldn't stop him. On two occasions he'd watched Wayne retrieve a key from under a terracotta plant pot balanced on the kitchen windowsill. There was nothing in it, not even a sprinkle of soil.

Stupid bugger.

He grabbed the key.

Click.

He froze. What the hell was that?

Something brushed past his leg, and he stepped back. A spurt of adrenaline surged into his bloodstream, rocketing his heart rate and making his muscles tremble.

Muffy!

"Fucking cat."

The annoying creature had come through the cat flap, and it had clicked shut. It stood there, staring up at him, feline eyes flashing and unblinking.

"Get out of here, or you'll end up meeting the same bad end as your master is about to."

The cat didn't move.

Mike sent a swift kick its way. Missed. The cat was quick and galloped around the side of the house and out of sight.

"Little shitty bastard," Mike muttered, letting himself into Wayne's kitchen. The appearance of Muffy had only served to remind Mike why he was here. Wayne had no respect for him or his garden.

And he was going to get what was coming to him.

Mike shut the door and flicked the lock; he didn't want to be disturbed.

They kitchen had an eerie glow owing to the full moon. It was messy—the sink full of mugs, plates, and pans and cooking debris spread out on every work surface.

He's as filthy as his cat.

Mike stepped up to a calendar. A black marker pen hung next to it, on a piece of string. He took the marker and slid it into his jeans pocket. He had a plan for that.

Wayne had one of those ugly knife holders, shaped like a person with holes for the knives to be stored in. Particularly tasteless, but a picture was forming in Mike's head about the kind of man he was dealing with here.

He plucked out a sharp vegetable knife and added it to his pocket along with the marker.

"What have we here?" he murmured, his gaze landing on a pile of carrots. "Bet you don't have to put up with cat shit on your veg, huh, but it's okay for me to."

He grabbed the biggest carrot and left the kitchen.

The hall had a golden glow, the lamppost outside invading the glass front door and creating an amber rectangle on the carpeted hall floor.

Mike stopped at the bottom of the stairs and looked up. Wayne still had his bedroom light on.

But that was okay.

Mike didn't mind waiting.

He was in no rush.

And wait he did.

And wait...and wait.

One hour later, just as Mike was contemplating going to finish Wayne off with the light still on, it finally went out.

Mike grinned. This is what he'd wanted. Dark. The way Muffy used his veg patch in the dark. It had to be then, didn't it, he'd notice the damn cat doing its business in the day.

He lifted each ankle in turn and rotated it. He'd become stiff standing at the bottom of the stairs for so long.

He then rolled out his shoulders and took a few deep breaths. Another ten minutes and it would be action time. He glanced at his watch. Just gone one in the morning.

Typical that Wayne was such a night owl. Mike could have been having fun with *her* all of this time.

Finally, ten minutes ticked round. His patience had run out; he'd just have to hope Wayne was asleep.

Cautiously, he went up the first step, crossing his fingers that his bulk wouldn't make it squeak.

It didn't.

He climbed higher still, gripping the carrot. The knife and pen in his pocket rubbed on his ass cheek.

When he reached the top, the excitement in his belly threatened to overcome him. It was swirling and cascading, gripping and releasing. This was his time now. His last chance to get revenge on those who'd wronged him.

Soon he'd be dead.

But Wayne would be dead sooner.

He opened the bedroom door and stood in the frame, surveying the bedroom.

A double bed stood in the middle, the tell-tale hump of Wayne's body at a slight angle beneath the duvet.

He was breathing slow and heavy, not quite snoring but probably would be soon...or would have been.

Mike stepped in and withdrew the vegetable knife from his back pocket. His stomach tightened then growled. A deep gurgling sound that barrelled through his guts.

Shit.

He clasped his abdomen and stared at Wayne.

Wayne moved his feet, then his shoulders. He grunted and turned to face Mike. His eyes flicked open, the whites flashing. "What the?" He propped up onto his elbows, the duvet slipping down his chest. "You!"

Mike rushed forward, knife held out. He moved fast, as if he were in the ring again, deceptively light on his feet for a man of his weight. He leapt onto the bed, straddling Wayne's torso and shoving the knife against his neck, right over the left jugular.

Wayne froze, eyes so wide Mike could see all of the whites now.

Wayne held his hands up, fingers splayed in a surrendering gesture. "Please."

"Not so cocky now, are you," Mike growled.

"What are you doing? Please…I'm sorry." Wayne swallowed, his Adam's apple scraping over the knife. "Really I am."

"You expect me to believe that?"

"Yes, honestly, I…" He shifted his hips as though testing the weight pinning him down.

"I'd keep really still if I were you." Mike's heart was swelling, and the rest of the world was fading away. The sense of control was intoxicating, as if he were drunk on power. Killing was an excellent way to spend his last days.

He jabbed the knife on Wayne's flesh a little harder. A drip of blood appeared.

Wayne let out a pathetic sob as the red trickle ran to the pillow.

"Your cat has no respect, and neither have you," Mike said.

"I do respect you." His voice shook. "And I'll keep the cat in, like you asked."

"Too late."

"Wh…what do you mean?"

"I mean it's too late. The time for doing the right thing has passed." Mike slid the knife around Wayne's neck, digging into the skin enough to make blood seep but not taking out any major vessels…yet.

Wayne snivelled. He really was a wimp of a man when it came down to it. The macho stuff was all show. He was brave when there was a fence between them.

Mike grinned, his cheeks balling his mouth had stretched so wide. With his free hand he reached for the marker pen and used his teeth to drag the lid off. He spat the lid onto the floor, a trail of spit going with it.

Wayne was shaking; his eyes flashed with terror.

"Try and relax," Mike said, using words he'd said to *her* earlier. "While I do what I need to."

"What? What are you going to do?"

Mike squeezed the knife closer.

"Ugh." Wayne arched his neck, trying but failing to get away from the sharp blade.

"I figured that since you like cats so much…" Mike placed the tip of the marker beside Wayne's right nostril. He dragged it over his cheek. He repeated the action, pleased with the thick dark lines on his pale skin. "…whiskers would suit you."

"Whiskers?"

"Yeah, whiskers." Mike added two more lines to Wayne's right cheek, then repeated the action on the other side.

"You're m…mad."

"Mad? Mmm, perhaps." He drew a small circle on the tip of Wayne's nose then blackened the centre. "I prefer to think of myself as just a dying bloke ticking things off my bucket list."

"Bucket list?" Mike's voice was barely a squeak. "This is on your bucket list?"

"Well, not *this* exactly, but getting even, that's something I want to do before I die. Right the wrongs, you know." He added a few more whiskers, just for fun. Wayne really did look a right prick now.

"My cat…shat in your veg patch. This is a bit extreme."

Mike tipped forward. This time he really did press hard over Wayne's jugular. "You see, it's the principle, Wayne the Pain. I asked you to make it stop..."

Wayne grunted, and he closed his eyes tight, the lashes meshing together.

"And you *didn't* make it stop. What the hell did you think I'd do? Just carry on eating shitty veg?"

"I'm sorry, and...I should have..."

"Yeah, you should have." Mike dragged the knife over the pulsing vein in Wayne's neck. He dug down deep, the blade slicing through the flesh easily, as if it were a perfectly cooked steak.

Instantly, blood arced from the hole. Mike was surprised how far it went. It really did spurt. The covers were soaked, as was Mike's leg on that side, his jeans absorbing the warm liquid.

He watched, fascinated.

Wayne gurgled and raised his head. He tried to push Mike away, but there was no strength behind the attempt—he was being drained of all power at an incredible rate.

Mike stayed seated over Wayne's body, holding him down as his life-force rushed from him. It was almost as though it was glad of the escape route. Would the ice-cream man's blood have been the same if he'd cut his throat, too? Mike would never know, but he'd always wonder. It was mesmerizing. A sight he'd never forget.

Still Wayne gurgled and twisted. He clutched his neck, and Mike let him. Nothing was going to stop the inevitable now. Death had opened its door and was welcoming him in.

Just like it would for Mike soon.

Wayne stilled. His hand flopped lifelessly to the bed.

Mike stared at him, the knife held forward. After his last victim having a go with a rock—Mike still had the bump on his head as a reminder—he wasn't taking any chances.

But Wayne was perfectly still. His chest didn't rise and fall beneath Mike, and his eyes were half open, staring at the curtains, unseeing.

"Bet you wish you'd been a better neighbour, eh?" Mike climbed off Wayne and drew the duvet back to reveal his naked body.

"Really? Never heard of fucking pyjamas?"

But it did make his next job easier. Mike held up the carrot. It was good and pointy, thick, too. Still with one eye on Wayne, just in case the bastard was faking it, he shoved Wayne's legs apart and then pushed the carrot up his arse. All the way. As far as it would go, so just the end with a tuft of leafy bits was sticking out.

He chuckled at the sight. What a humiliation, and a fitting end when he thought crap went so well with veg.

Chapter Eight

"Ma'am I know you're busy with the ice-cream murder but I thought you might like to know about this?"

Shona looked from the whiteboard to Andy. "No problem, what's up?"

He consulted his smart phone. "Darren just reported a missing person?"

"Who?" Earle asked, biting into a carrot cupcake and getting frosting on the tip of his nose. He'd brought a tin of them in that morning. Delicious.

"A Tammy Robin."

"Who called it in?" Shona glanced at Earle who'd stopped chewing. They knew Tammy. She had a bit of a thing for Earle. Wore the shortest shorts and the tightest tops whenever he was around. Or maybe she wore them all the time, Shona didn't know.

"A Mrs Robin, her mother. You've had contact before, haven't you?"

"Yes." Shona took a lip balm from her pocket and applied it. "Complaints about garden gnomes being stolen."

"Not a job for the serious crime unit then." Andy raised his eyebrows.

"No, not exactly." Earle huffed. "A waste of police time if you ask me."

"A crime is a crime." Shona spoke fast to deflect attention from Earle. He'd never had any patience for Tammy's flirting. "When was she last seen?"

"Yesterday afternoon. She went for lunch, as usual, at Mrs Robin's then left, promising to be back at lunchtime today. No-show."

"Mobile?"

"No answer."

"She's a grown woman," Earle said. "Perhaps she had other things to do."

"It's a possibility." Shona frowned. "But she struck me as a devoted daughter. If her plan had been to go for lunch as usual, it's odd she didn't turn up." She glanced at her watch. "And you know what they say, the first seventy-two hours are the most critical for a missing person. I suggest we pay Mrs Robin a visit while we wait for forensics to come back on Barry White's case."

Earle wiped cake crumbs from the corner of his mouth with a tissue. "If you think that's for the best."

"I do." Shona pointed at his nose

He swiped the frosting off.

She nodded at Andy. "Can you take a quick break from checking Barry's social media and do an ANPR on Tammy Robin's car. We have the registration, right? And check her phone's last ping if you can."

"Of course. Let's hope the car has been picked up on one of the main roads." He stood and shook his head. "The sooner we get more cameras the better."

"I agree." Shona grabbed one of Earle's cakes. "This'll have to be lunch."

"Guilt free. It's wholemeal flour and lots of carrots." He grinned.

"One of my five a day, eh?"

"I wouldn't go that far." He laughed.

Half an hour later, they pulled up at Mrs Robin's house for the second time in as many months.

The gnomes still stood in the front garden, baking in the heat, and the shrubs had had a good prune—some of them appeared the worse for wear after their meeting with the shears.

Shona knocked on the door.

Mrs Robin answered it within a minute. "Police?"

"Yes, Mrs Robin. I'm DI Shona Williams, and this is DS Earle Montague. We met a while ago regarding missing gnomes." She gestured at the garden.

"Ah yes, of course, I remember. Tammy called you about that." She looked at Earle. "No idea why...maybe I do." Shaking her head, she turned. "Come in. I'll put the kettle on."

"Thank you." Shona went in.

Earle followed and closed the door.

"When did you last see your daughter?" Shona asked as she stepped into the kitchen.

"Yesterday, she came for lunch, she always does in the week. She works a regular late shift, see, at Nightingale Care Home. Says she likes old people; that's just as well." She rubbed the back of her veiny hands. "Since that's what I am."

"Did she turn up for work yesterday evening?"

"No." A worried frown ploughed over Mrs Robin's brow. "That's why I called you. After she didn't show up here, I called her mobile. Straight to voicemail. Naturally, I left a message for her, telling her I was worried. Then I rang the care home. They said she hadn't shown up and they'd been unable to reach her." She pressed her hand to her chest. "That's when I really started to worry. Even if she'd been in an accident she'd have called, if she could have, or you...you folk would have been round to tell me the worst."

"We haven't heard anything to that effect." Shona rested her hand on Mrs Robin's forearm. Poor soul was ready to spill tears.

"And has she ever done anything like this before?" Earle asked, his pen hovering over his small black notepad.

"No, nothing...well, once, as a teenager, she ran off to her friend's house when we'd had an argument about her makeup. She wore it heavy even back then. But Jude, that was her friend's mum, called to say she was there, so I wasn't worried."

"So it's out of character," Earle asked.

"Very. Out of all my four children, Tammy is here visiting the most. She's my rock, she really is. I'm guessing it's because she doesn't have a fella and kids of her own yet and..." She squeezed her eyes closed and gulped down a sob.

"We'll find her," Shona said. "And I'm sure there's a simple explanation."

"What time did she leave here yesterday?" Earle asked.

"About two, I think...but there was one weird thing."

"What's that?" Shona studied Mrs Robin.

"She said goodbye and let herself out. I didn't think anything else of it. But when I went into the living room, an hour later, to change the water in my roses, pretty bunch they are from my son, her car was still there?"

Earle raised his eyebrows. "And she would normally have driven away in it?"

"Well, yes, it's a long walk otherwise."

"So what did you think?" Shona asked.

"I wondered if she'd gone to the towpath, to collect brambles. It's a bit early really, but she does that, most years. My Tammy makes the best jam, she really does."

"And had she said that's what she was going to do?"

"No, that's what's odd. She would have, usually. We, I, don't have much to chat about so we discuss the small stuff, if you know what I mean."

Shona nodded. "But the car isn't there now?"

"No, when I looked out at four it had gone. So she must have come back to get it."

Or someone had.

"Do you have her mobile number?" Earle asked.

"Yes, of course." The kettle came to the boil. Mrs Robin ignored it. "Here it is." She tapped the screen of an old phone. "Ready?"

"Yes."

She read it out.

Earle wrote it down. Shona dialled it on her own phone.

"Still voicemail." Shona ended the call.

"That's what I got." Mrs Robin wrung her hands.

"I'll get our tech guys on it, see if they can pinpoint where it was last used."

"They can do that?"

"Yes, ma'am, they can." Shona smiled and handed over a card. "And in the meantime, I want you to call me if she turns up or you think of anything else."

Mrs Robin took it. "Yes, of course I will." She paused. "Oh, I hope she does turn up soon. I'm so worried. My poor, sweet little Tammy." She shook her head and downturned her mouth.

"Try not to worry, it won't help, but if you remember anything at all that you think *will* help, call me."

She nodded. "Of course."

Shona stepped back onto the street, Earle at her side. "What do you think?"

"She might have met a fella and be holed up with him."

"She only has eyes for you." As Shona had said it she wished she hadn't.

But instead of a cutting remark, Earle chuckled. "She's barking up the wrong tree."

Shona smiled, but it quickly dropped. "If we hadn't met Tammy and can attest to the fact she's devoted to her mum, I'd be less worried. But Mrs Robin is right, this is out of character. And not to turn up for work at a care home."

"And what's all this about the car being outside after she'd gone?"

"Weird, right?"

"Very." He nodded at the towpath. "Shall we take a wander?"

"Good idea."

They walked down the small quiet street. Most drives were empty, indicating people were out at work. When they passed through the gap in the houses that led to the canal, they passed a woman with a terrier. A fluffy grey cat sat high on the fence staring at the dog as it barked up at it.

The canal was still and the sides of the towpath heavy with nettles. "Can't see any brambles for picking, can you?" Shona said.

"No, nothing." Earle batted a bug away from his face. "Now what?"

"A few door-to-doors won't hurt."

"We could get uniform to do that."

"No, we're here now and…"

"What?"

"I dunno, it feels kind of personal. I like Tammy. I like her mum, too."

"Yeah, I know what you mean." He turned. "I'll take the right side, you take the left?"

"Yes, that's fine, we'll soon have it done."

They split up and started knocking. The first two doors Shona went to gave her zilch, no one home. The third presented a harassed mum with a baby in her arms and a toddler hanging from her skirt. She'd seen nothing out of the ordinary the day before and had spent the afternoon at a kid's soft play.

The next house was also empty, but while Shona was standing at the door, the grey cat came and coiled itself around her ankles. "Hey, cutie," she said. "Where do you live?" It was extra pretty, exotic, a fancy breed. It had a collar on, with a phone number.

When there was no answer, Shona moved to the next house. The room to the left of the door had the curtains closed. In the other window, the flickering of a TV, through the nets, gave her confidence someone was home. Which was good because as this living room was almost opposite Mrs Robin's house, there was a good chance this person had seen something.

She rang the doorbell again, frustration rising when it seemed no one was going to answer. Then the slide of a chain and the click of a lock.

The door opened.

A man stood there, mid-fifties, she reckoned. He was tall with wide shoulders and a beefy neck, though he had dark circles under his eyes, and his lips were cracked. He had a few nasty scratches on his cheek.

"Good afternoon, I'm DI Shona Williams."

"DI?"

"Detective Inspector."

He tugged on a dry bit of lip skin with his top teeth and glanced over his shoulder. "What do you want?"

"I'm investigating the disappearance of Miss Tammy Robin. Her mother lives opposite."

"I don't know where she is." He pushed the door up a fraction.

Shona studied his eyes. There was something dull about them, a lack of light in their depths. "What's your name?"

"Why?"

She smiled, trying to give the impression of patience. "Because I'm a police officer and I'm asking you."

"Mike. Mike Mendes."

"Mr Mendes, I'm trying to find out what time Miss Robin left this street yesterday."

"What do you mean?"

"What time she drove away."

"How would I know?"

"Well, it's just..." She pointed to his window then across the road. "If you have a habit of watching TV in the afternoon then maybe you would have noticed."

"I didn't."

"So you were out at work yesterday?"

"I don't work." He rubbed at the scratch, poking a small scab.

"You don't?"

"No, I'm dying. Got the Big C. Won't see Christmas, they said."

"Oh." She inclined her head. "I'm very sorry to hear that." No wonder he had dark circles under his eyes.

"Not your fault."

"But still. I'm sorry." She pointed to his cheek. "How'd you get those scratches, if you don't mind me asking?"

"There's a bloody annoying cat around here. I helped it get down from my tree, it was stuck, see. Little bastard scratched me for my trouble."

"Not very grateful, but I'm sure the owner is."

He huffed.

"So you didn't see Tammy Robin yesterday? Or her car?"

Again he glanced over his shoulder.

"Am I keeping you from something?" Shona asked.

"No, I…actually, I have some pasta boiling. Got hungry for some. Don't deny myself these days, what's the point?"

She smiled.

"No." He shook his head. "I didn't see her or her car. Sometimes do, but not yesterday."

"Okay, well, thank you for your time, Mr Mendes. I appreciate it. And take care of yourself."

"The time for that has gone." He shrugged. "Best thing I can do now is tick off the things on my bucket list and hope for a peaceful end."

Chapter Nine

Mike slipped the chain into place, locked the door, and rushed to the living room. He poked his finger around the nets and stared outside.

Bloody nosy policewoman had bugged the hell out of him. Anger raced around his veins, probably spreading the cancer further and faster, knocking days off what he had left.

There was a man with her now, a huge bloke, black, looked like the sort Mike had met in the ring a few times…years ago. They were pointing up and down the street, talking. She gestured his way then tapped her cheek as though describing his scratches.

Scratches that bitch upstairs had given him.

He flicked the net curtain back and stormed from the room. But instead of going upstairs he went into the kitchen. Second drawer down, beneath the hob, was his nan's old wooden rolling pin. Stained from use and with a split in it. He grabbed it and paced into the dining room.

He had to do something. Use up the fury, burn the red-rage, he needed to expend it somehow. If he didn't he'd kill *her*, and she was too much fun alive. Not like the stupid ice-cream man, or Wayne the Pain, they were better off dead. But *her*…she still had entertainment value.

Once in the dining room, he glared at the gnomes. The one nearest to him had a red pointed hat, a white beard, and held a watering can.

Mike smashed the rolling pin down on its head. The clay shattered easily, fragments spraying this way and that. The face had imploded.

He whacked it again, taking out the torso. Shards of the shiny black watering can bounced off the wall.

The next gnome had podgy thumbs hooked into a shiny black belt and had its head back, eyes closed, laughing.

"I'll wipe that smile from your face." Mike took a sideways swing, taking the head clean off. It rolled to the floor then under the dining table.

Mike gritted his teeth and swung at the next, then the next. It felt good, to be destroying. His wrath had an outlet. The gnomes were weak and pathetic.

When he'd finished smashing the last one into hundreds of pieces, he stood straight and let the rolling pin hang at his side. He was out of breath, and his heart thundered along at a clapping rate. But at least the fury of having the police turn up at his house had gone.

Just like they have?

He peered out of the closed curtains.

The big four-by-four was nowhere to be seen.

"And stay away," he muttered, dropping the rolling pin to the floor.

He slipped his hand down his trousers, stroked himself. While his pecker still worked, he wanted to keep *her* cuffed to the bed. Having the police take *her* away just wouldn't do. Not one bit. But he felt confident they had nothing on him. They'd asked for his help after all. Had he seen anything? Not a chance.

And *her* car...it would be weeks before anyone found that. He'd hidden it in such an isolated spot and made sure there were none of his fingerprints on it.

After Mike had enjoyed *her* for a while, he went into the bathroom, the only other room on the first floor that faced the back of the house. He opened the window and examined Wayne the Pain's house.

The bedroom curtains were still closed. There was no movement, nothing to suggest his body had been found.

How long will it be until someone notices he's missing?

Mike chuckled. It was a bit like a test, wasn't it. To see how loved you were. The length of time until someone worried was the barometer.

Hadn't taken Tammy long to be missed. But he got that. She was hot, sexy, and quite a catch.

Literally.

But Wayne, he was a smug arsehole. Could be weeks or months until anyone bothered to check on him. And by then...well, what would it matter to Mike?

Movement by Wayne's back door caught his eye.

The bloody cat. Muffy.

It went through the cat flap, and Mike chuckled some more. A sudden visual jumped into his brain of the cat eating Wayne. The way they said dogs did when their owners died. Perhaps it would start by licking at the blood, then nibbling at his tongue which had been protruding. Going for the eyeballs next and then maybe his cock.

Oh, how Mike would love to see that. He'd have to keep an eye on Muffy, see if she had blood on her pale fur. If she did, it might even be worth risking going back into Wayne's house for a look, just to satisfy his curiosity.

Mike closed the window and headed out of the bathroom. But standing at the top of the stairs a sudden, wicked, sharp pain pierced his right side.

"Ah, fuck." He gripped his torso, just below his ribs, as the pain seemed to tighten every organ in his body. "Shit." He screwed up his eyes and held his breath, hoping the wave of agony would pass.

He'd felt this before. It was why he'd gone to the doctors in the first place. A few scans later, they'd found the Big C.

On and on he was tortured as he stood at the top of the stairs. He tried to breathe through it, counted to ten, twenty, thirty, hoping it would be gone by the time he made it to one hundred.

Finally, it began to ease, and the mean band loosened. He staggered to the bathroom again and opened the cabinet, reached for a bottle of codeine.

"Bugger it." The thing was empty.

He tossed it behind himself. It landed in the bath with a clatter.

"Where are you?" He was sure he had more. He had to have. This was the sort of thing he was careful about.

But there were no more codeine capsules. Plenty of other stuff for nausea, constipation, and indigestion, but no good, strong pain relief.

He managed to get down the stairs, sweat pricking his brow. There was only one thing for it, he'd have to get himself to the pharmacy and buy some. It was a ten-minute walk to the parade of shops on Cory Road. It was getting late, but they should still be open.

He grabbed his wallet from the side cabinet then unchained and unlocked the door.

Trying to stand straight, he released his grip on his side and locked up. His steps were faltering as he walked down his garden path, but by the time he reached the pavement, the pain was definitely receding. He imagined it like a tide. When it was in, at full tide, it was unbearable, all-consuming. He could do nothing, think of nothing. But when it ebbed away, he became himself again. A functioning adult male.

He walked slowly but steadily in the direction of Cory. He tried not to think of the pain being there all the time. But he wasn't stupid. He knew the agony would be with him in the end, the Big C his only companion while he gasped his last breath.

It took him longer to get to the pharmacy than he'd hoped. The number forty-two had gone past, meaning it really was getting late.

The green cross came into view, and he hurried a little, feeling stronger now, the Big C asleep once more.

When he reached it, a man stepped out wearing a pale-blue summer jacket. He had a moustache, one of those ridiculous ones that were pointy at the ends. He locked the door.

"Hey, excuse me," Mike called, breaking into a jog. "I need something."

The man turned and withdrew the key. "I'm sorry, we're closed."

"But..." Mike came to halt. "I've ran out of codeine. And I've got this pain, cancer, see. I could really do with you opening up again."

"No can do." He shook his head and pocketed the keys.

"Er, yeah, you *can* do. Keys." He pointed at the man's open jacket, spotting the name badge on his shirt, *Rufus Drake, Head Pharmacist.* "Door." He gestured to the lock. "Rufus."

"No, sorry, it's on a timer, the alarm." He pulled up the zipper on his jacket then glanced at his watch. "Comes on at exactly six and will be that way until nine tomorrow morning. Anything sets it off in the meantime and the police arrive."

"What?"

"I'm sorry, drugs are frequently targeted by unscrupulous individuals, I'm sure you can appreciate that." With each word his moustache twitched, the little ends jabbing upwards.

"So key in the number." Mike frowned. He really didn't fancy going home without codeine. Okay, the pain had taken a hike, but there was no knowing when it would show its ugly face again.

"I'm sorry, I'm not at liberty to do that."

"So I just have to be in agony," Mike snapped. "Some fucking pharmacist you are."

"Please do not use that tone with me." He'd spoken sternly, but a flash of wariness had crossed over his eyes.

Mike liked that.

"Are you fucking dying, Rufus, eh?" Mike loomed over the man. "You any idea what it's like to be being eaten alive from the inside out?"

"Perhaps if you get to the Tesco, over at Rygate, their pharmacy will help you out. They're open until eight, I believe."

"Rygate? How the fuck do you suggest I get there?"

The pharmacist stepped away. "Car? Bus?"

Mike's ears buzzed. A familiar mist descended over his peripheral vision. This idiot was supposed to be a health care professional, there was a clue in the name, *care*, and he clearly didn't. "You're a tosser, you know that."

"Goodbye, sir. We're open again at nine, I can see to you then." There was a slight shake to his voice.

"You could help me now if you really wanted to." Mike glared at him. He was small-framed and skinny; his legs were bowed as if he'd spent too long riding a horse.

Rufus didn't answer but walked parallel to the parade of shops, passing a hairdresser's, nail salon, betting shop, and a tired Spar.

Mike clenched and unclenched his fists. The pharmacist had a bad attitude. He was one of those jobsworth twats. What a load of nonsense that the alarm was on a timer. What happened if there was a customer in the shop at six and it took a few minutes to serve them? The police had to show? Of course not. The man was a blatant liar. How often had he done this?

Mike slunk along after him.

A couple of girls in high heels came out of the nail salon, their arms linked, giggling. A drunk geezer wandered into the betting shop holding a can of Tennent's.

Mike veered around him, then, when the pharmacist went from view, he quickened his pace.

The rubbish truck rattled past, creating a right din. Mike followed the pharmacist around the side of the parade. Here, litter had gathered, and the kerb was broken. He avoided a pile of dog sick.

Where's he going?

It soon became clear. Around the back of the parade was a small car park, for staff presumably, because it had a flimsy barrier blocking it from the side access. There were no windows overlooking it, and a row of huge wheelie bins stood to the left beside a tall wooden fence.

There was only one car. A small red Fiesta parked right next to the bins.

The pharmacist was heading towards it.

Mike broke into a jog, relieved when the pain didn't bite his side.

I have to get to him before he reaches his car.

Rufus turned at the sound of Mike's footsteps. There was real, undisguised alarm on his face.

"Wait," Mike called.

"I can't help you." He fumbled with his keys.

"Clearly." Mike reached him.

Rufus put his hand on his car door. Yanked the handle.

Mike banged it closed, reconnecting it with the frame.

"I say," Rufus gasped, "that's really not appropriate."

"About as appropriate as you being a shithead," Mike snarled.

"Please, step away."

"Why should I? You wouldn't do what I wanted you to do for me."

"It wasn't a case of not wanting to, I—ugh!"

Mike withdrew his fist from the man's abdomen and watched him double over then stagger against the car. He hadn't held back, had given him a real weighty gut punch.

"Please, no…here…take the keys."

"What good are they if the alarm will go off?" Mike stepped close again. "You think I look like an idiot, Rufus?"

"No. No, of course not." He shook his head and tried to straighten, still gripping his side.

"Not nice, is it? Pain." Mike tutted. "Now you know why I need the fucking painkillers."

"I'll drive you to Tesco. G…g…get in, won't take long."

"Too little too late." Mike shook his head. "Sorry."

"Sorry for what?"

"This." Mike belted him again, in the chest this time. Like with the ice-cream man, Mike's entire body rejoiced in overpowering his opponent. It was a snapshot into the good old days. He thumped Rufus in the face, over his ridiculous moustache.

His lip split, and he yelped.

"Shut up." Mike swept his attention around. The place was still deserted.

"No, no…please. Leave me…alone…"

"Why should I?" Mike hung over him. He really was a pathetically scrawny creature. Twig-like arms and legs, and a neck as scraggy as a skinny chicken. It was a very one-sided battle. Like a featherweight taking on a heavyweight.

But hey ho. Mike didn't make the rules.

"Help! Help!" The pharmacist wailed.

"I said shut it." Mike spun the man around then hooked him into a headlock. He placed his free palm on Rufus's temple.

The man went quiet and stopped struggling. As if sensing the acute danger of his position, he gripped Mike's forearm.

Mike was breathing fast, excitement a real physical presence surrounding them, stroking the air, filling his lungs. He held this man's life in his hands. One twist and shove, and his neck would break matchstick-style. Mike had never done that to anyone, but he'd always wanted to. It was a bucket list thing.

"Goodnight," he said, then yanked his arm one way and pushed the other with his palm.

The crack was sharp, like a glass hitting a tiled floor, or a stone colliding with the blade of a lawnmower. And the effect was instant.

Rufus's legs went limp, and his arms dangled. His weight hung heavy and dead.

"Wow, that was easy," Mike muttered. "Hardly any resistance." Perhaps there would have been on a bigger man. Mike didn't know. But he'd done it now. Ticked the box, and the stupid pharmacist had deserved it.

But now what...?

He glanced to the right, spotted the wheelie bins. Quickly, he half dragged, half carried the body over to the black one. Household waste. That should do it. No one ever looked in there.

This dead body was light in comparison to the fat bastard ice-cream man, that had been a real struggle to get him into the freezer, but it had been worth it. What a sight he'd been, all folded in.

Mike threw Rufus's body upwards. It landed belly over the lip of the bin. Mike shoved at his feet—fancy brown leather shoes—and poked him in. He then shut the lid.

Evidence destroyed.

Or at least it was hidden for now. Maybe the dustmen wouldn't even notice and he'd go into the crusher and be mincemeat spread out on all the stinky rubbish.

His disappearance would be a mystery, a bit like Tammy's.

Mike swiped his palms together and went back to the car. The door was still open. There was a pen on the passenger seat. Mike itched to write a note, in Portuguese, but there was no paper. He glanced around, spotted a piece of white card on the ground.

He grabbed it, then reached for the pen, being careful not to touch anything in the car.

A vida é curta viva.

Chapter Ten

Earle sat heavily on his chair and rubbed his temples.

"Morning, partner," Shona said with a frown. "You okay?"

"Yeah."

"Sure?"

"Didn't sleep well."

"Really? Thought you were out for the count every night without fail. Eight hours."

"Not last night."

"Why?"

He glanced around and shrugged.

"Earle?"

"I just felt…" He sighed.

"What?"

"It's dumb."

"No, it's not." She leaned forward. "What is it?"

"I thought I heard something, as I was dropping off, about eleven."

"Something?"

"I dunno, just a bump, a creak downstairs."

"And, was it anything?"

"Of course not, and I did look. But…" He tapped his chest. "My adrenaline was going then, I couldn't get off to sleep. It was like my mind had gone into overdrive."

"Badger?"

He closed his eyes and squeezed the bridge of his nose. "Stupid, isn't it."

"Not at all, he's very likely taken a pop at your ex-partner, made a very real threat to you in the form of a note at his sentencing."

"We don't know if he's even in Ironash, and how would he know where I live?"

"That sort of thing isn't hard to find out." She stood and rested her hand on his shoulder. "I'll get Andy to check he has a parole officer allocated and keep any eye on CCTV, see if he shows up."

"Do you think that's necessary?"

"Yes, I do." Her phone rang. "Darren?"

"Just took a message from SOCO. Tammy Robin's car has been found."

"Really? Where?" She grabbed a pen and held it poised over her notebook.

"Ealing Woods. Dog handling officers found it when they were doing a search of the area as part of the Barry White case."

"Ice-cream man."

"Yep, it's about five hundred yards away, half submerged."

"Are SOCO onto it? We need to know if there was anyone else in the car with her."

"I believe so but I can check."

"Thanks. Do that." She hung up.

"Tammy's car?" Earle said.

"Ealing Woods. Pretty big coincidence, don't you think?"

"Yeah, but no idea how they'd be connected."

"One thing is for sure, if her car is hidden and half drowned, it's because she's being kept hidden somewhere, too." She gestured to Andy to join them.

He came over, holding a clipboard and pen. "Yes, ma'am."

"A few things. One, can you keep an eye out for Udall Hicks, otherwise known as Badger. He's finished his time at Her Majesty's pleasure, and we need a release address if he has one. Start with parole."

"You think he's in Ironash?" He wrote on his clipboard.

"I don't know, but we need to know. And did you find anything on CCTV regarding Tammy Robin's car?"

"I did, was just about to show you." He set a grainy photograph on the table.

They all studied it.

"Is that her driving?" Shona asked.

"I'm not sure." Earle rubbed his forehead. "Looks kind of big, broad-shouldered."

"I agree. Can you zoom in some more, Andy?"

"That's as close as I can get it." Andy clicked his tongue on the roof of his mouth. "All I can say for certain is this was taken at four fifteen on the day of her disappearance."

"Where?" Earle asked.

"Six Mile Lane."

"On the way to Ealing Woods. Makes sense." Shona nodded.

"Ealing Woods?" Andy asked.

"The car has just been found there."

"I'm guessing minus Miss Robin?" he said.

"As far as we can tell at the moment." She gestured to Earle. "We should get down there, suss it out."

"I agree."

"Andy, can you organise a door-to-door on the Whilton Estate. And not just the street Mrs Robin lives on, but the ones either side and opposite. Someone might have seen something, and I want them asked while it's fresh in their memories." She shook her head. "It's the last place she was seen, we have nothing else to go on. Oh, and get a picture of her, the officers can use that. We forgot yesterday, maybe because we both know what she looks like already." Her heart sagged. Mrs Robin would be even more worried when she heard about the car being found. "We should pop in later, to her mother, Earle."

"I agree, but better still, we should find her daughter."

Within minutes, they were heading along Six Mile Lane. Shona really hoped they'd get a clue from the car. Leads were slim pickings at the moment, and that wasn't doing them any favours when time was of the essence.

A uniform directed them past the Barry White murder site, which was now strung up with police tape. When they spotted the SOCO van along a dirt track, they drew up behind it.

"Creepy place, these woods." Shona pulled a face as she slipped on protectives. "Its like the light can't get through the trees."

"Yeah, it's even denser than where we were yesterday, near the other murder site."

"Other?"

"Fuck. I hope she's not been murdered." Earle suppressed a shudder.

"Me, too, the poor soul."

He glanced over his shoulder. "What was that?"

"What?"

"Shit. That." He pointed into the gloom.

Shona followed his line of sight. "I think it's a bird. A jay...they're a flash of blue and pink."

The high-pitched *cack, cack, cack* of a jay bounced around the trees.

"Oh, okay." Earle sighed.

"Shit, you've got a bad case of the jitters."

"I know." He ran his hand over his short hair. "And it's not like me, not at all."

"So lets find him and bring him in?"

"On what grounds?"

She had no answer to that.

"See."

"We'll think of something, once we've sorted out this particular crazy. Come on."

They followed the sound of voices and tyre tracks and soon came across Julie and her forensic team.

"Hey," Shona said.

Julie withdrew from where she'd been stooped by the driver's door. "Oh, hi, DI, DS. You're keeping me busy, what with the frozen corpse yesterday and now this."

"Sorry about that." Shona smiled.

"Ha, not your fault, it's the murdering bastards of Ironash."

"Which are luckily in a minority."

"I dunno, seems to be a frequent event this summer."

"We're very much hoping this isn't a murder scene. What can you make of it so far?"

She held up a pair of tweezers and a small plastic bag. "Luckily the back of the driver's seat isn't underwater, though I wouldn't be surprised if it went that way. I reckon this is some kind of bloody sink hole."

"What's in the bag?" Earle asked.

"Oh, yes, some black fibres, I've taped them off. We found some on Barry White, too, so if they're the same..."

"The cases are connected."

"Exactly."

She pointed at the ground. "We've lifted a few boot marks, too, big ones."

"Any at the other scene?" Shona asked.

"A few partials." She shrugged. "It's much wetter here. But we might be able to get a match."

"Any..." Earle paused. "Any blood?"

"No, nothing to suggest there's been a murder, just the dumping of a car."

"You think there's any chance it was her driving it here?" Shona asked Earle.

"No, I really don't, that just didn't look like her, did it?"

Shona shook her head. "So where is she?" Her phone rang. "Andy, anything?"

"Sergeant Nicols just called in from the Whilton Estate."

"Yes?"

"She was doing door-to-door on Sisley Street, the one adjacent to Mrs Robins, and she's found another one."

"Another one?"

"Another body?"

"What?" Shona's mouth fell open, and she held her hands wide. She looked up at Earle. "Another body."

He puffed up his cheeks and blew out a breath.

"Yeah, she was knocking on number twelve, and a woman bustled up the path in a right state. Said her son lived there and he hadn't been answering his phone so she'd come to check on him. Let herself in then started hollering. He'd had his throat cut in the bed."

"Jesus Christ. Okay, we're on our way, and I'll let Julie know, I'm with her now. Get the place cordoned off so SOCO can do their job."

"I'm sure Nicols is on the case but I'll double-check."

Shona ended the call. "Julie, are you nearly done here?"

She sighed. "I got the gist of that. Another one?"

"Afraid so, over at the Whilton Estate, which is where the owner of this car was last seen. There's something fishy going on, that's for sure."

"I agree. My new colleague, Kyle, will have to take that. I've barely started here."

"No problem."

"He's a highly qualified forensic scientist, just done a PhD. Always trust the science, right."

Shona smiled. She also trusted her gut instinct and she'd bet good money that Tammy, Barry White, and this new case were all connected. But how?

Sisley Street was full of marked cars when they arrived, plus Ironash's second SOCO van. Nicols had a log on the go and was standing at the end of the path that led to number twelve.

"Sergeant," Shona said, after putting on yet another set of protectives and walking over to her. "What's the situation?"

"Hello, ma'am. The victim's mother has been taken to her sister's house, over the other side of town. The deceased's name is Wayne Farthing, thirty-one years old. I did ask her if she knew of anyone who might want to hurt her son. She said no, that he was a nice bloke, had loads of friends, played for Ironash footy team, and worked as a sparky."

"Okay, good thinking. Are SOCO up there now?"

"Yes, but not Julie Summers, a guy I haven't seen before. They're upstairs."

"Julie's busy at Ealing Woods." Shona signed the log.

Earle followed suit.

They went into the house and straight up the stairs which were directly opposite the front door.

"Who is that?" a deep voice called down.

"DI Williams and DS Montague," Shona called.

"Oh, okay, come up."

They went into the room opposite the top of the stairs. A youngish man in a white protective was directing a similarly dressed police photographer.

"Shit," Shona muttered, taking in the sight on the bed.

A man lay in a pool of dark blood. His throat had been hacked, and tendons, veins, and skin were dangling like a piece of material that had been scissored. His face was really weird, as if it had been drawn on. But what got Shona the most was his akimbo legs. His cock lay flaccid on dark pubic hair, and from beneath his balls, a sprout of green and a flash of orange.

"Is that a...?" Earle peered forward.

"Carrot in his arse," the SOCO said. "Aye, it is." He nodded at each of them in turn. "I'm Kyle McFarlane, new around here."

"Nice to meet you," Shona said, grimacing as she studied the carrot top. "Wish it could have been under better circumstances."

"Well, at least you won't forget our first meeting." Kyle chuckled.

"I guess." She scanned the room. "What's that?"

On a glossy white cupboard door was a scrawl of red writing.

Respeitar a vida, respeitar um ao outro.

"What does that say?" she said.

"Respect life, respect each other." Kyle didn't look up from what he was doing. "In Portuguese."

"You speak it?" Earle asked.

"No, I used Google translate when I saw it."

"Another cryptic Portuguese message," Shona said. "Just like at the last scene."

"Means we're definitely searching for the same person," Earle said.

Shona nodded. "I agree, but what's the Portuguese connection? It's not like Ironash has a big population from there."

"Perhaps he, or she, doesn't speak English." Earle shrugged.

"I don't think it's a she. Barry White can't have been easy to put in that freezer."

"Freezer?" Kyle finally looked up. "Nice."

"What?" Shona asked.

"That'll make for an interesting autopsy, you know."

Whatever floats his boat.

"That should cover everything." The photographer lowered his camera. "I'll be off now. Ma'am, sir." He stepped past Shona and Earle and left the room.

"Cause of death," Kyle said, wafting his hand over the deceased, "cut to the major vessels of the throat and subsequent hypovolemia. I'd say about twelve hours ago, give or take. I'll know more when I get him back to the table."

"What the hell is going on around here?" Shona stepped up to the bed and studied the dead man's face. "What's this? Whiskers or something?"

"Seems like it." Earle nodded.

"And a nose." Kyle hovered his gloved finger over the round black circle on the end of the victim's nose. "Could be a cat or a rabbit maybe."

Shona had a sudden image of the fluffy pale-grey cat winding around her legs the day before, when she'd been doing door-to-door not far from here.

"Cat face. Carrots. It doesn't make sense." Earle nibbled on his bottom lip, his brow furrowed in a thought frown.

"No, it doesn't...but it must somehow." She walked to the window and opened the curtain.

Outside was a neat lawned garden, though there appeared to be a limp lettuce, uprooted, lying in the centre. The borders were plain, just mud, and a single pot with a few weeds in it sat beside a small patio area. "He's not a big gardener."

"He *wasn't*," Kyle said.

"Mmm." Shona studied the house directly behind. Within it grew a large silver birch, planted a bit too close to the house in her opinion, because some of the branches stroked the brickwork. One in particular touched the sill of a window with a drawn down black blind.

Movement downstairs, seemed to be a kitchen as there was a tap visible, caught her attention. It was a bloke, big, and she realised it was the man with the scratches on his cheek she'd spoken to the day before. Mike Mendes, yes, that was it. Although he hadn't seen Tammy Robin leave her mother's, perhaps he'd spotted something odd going on in the house behind.

"Earle, let's go knock on the door of that guy again. The one I told you about with the cat scratches. He lives right just over the fence.

"Cat scratches." Earle studied the body again. "Cat whiskers, nose...you think there's a link?"

She blew out a breath. "No idea...it's a weird one."

"Aren't they all?"

Shona smiled at Kyle. "Let me know if you find anything. I've got bodies backing up like lemmings waiting to jump today."

"That's why I'm here, help mop up the mess." He put a thermometer away. "You're very young to be a DI."

Shona was a little taken aback by his abruptness. She was settling into Ironash, and it had been a while since she'd had a comment about her age or her looks.

"Er, I'm sorry," he said, his cheeks flushing a little. "Not known for my social graces. Scientific mind, see."

"No worries." She smiled; he was clearly ruffled. "I worked hard, focused, got to where I wanted to go with single-minded, bloody determination."

"I admire that."

She didn't miss the fact that he glanced at her ring finger.

She quashed down the urge to check out his. She wasn't interested. She was with Ben…kind of. Not quite into boyfriend territory yet, but they were getting there. Which reminded her, she really needed to knock off on time and get herself to the dojo. It would do her good after the grizzly sights in the woods and in this room.

Chapter Eleven

Mike rubbed his right side. The pain was still there, but duller now. After he'd offed the pain-in-the-arse pharmacist, he'd taken a cab to the Tesco over on Rygate—sod the expense—and got some codeine.

He'd knocked back two tablets and slept as though he was practicing for being dead. The oblivion had been a treat, but it had taken him a while to get going throughout the morning. He'd had a failed attempt at pleasure with *her*, slapped her pathetic tear-stained face a few times for not helping the situation—there could be some enthusiasm—then cooked beans on toast and eaten a packet of fancy chocolate biscuits.

And now, as *Loose Women* ended, he felt considerably better. Maybe he'd be able to get it up later. Make the most of having access to *her*. He wouldn't live forever, after all.

He huffed at that and glanced out the front window. All was quiet at Mrs Robin's house. No more nancy-pancy police officers visiting, thank goodness. They could go and take a running jump; they needed to stay out of his hair.

His attention landed on the stupid gnomes in her front garden. God, he hated them. Perhaps he should take them all. That way he wouldn't have to spend his last days with them in his line of sight.

Yeah, that was what he'd do. He'd go and get them. Now. There was no one around. He'd bold as brass nick them and chuck them in the dining room with the others. What did it matter? Plus, old Mrs Robin would be so strung out on her missing daughter she wouldn't give a hoot about gnomes.

Mike pulled on his black sweater, boots, and after guzzling a glass of water, he unchained and unlocked the door.

The still-warm air washed over him, and the scent of roses and mown grass flitted up his nose. Damn, he'd miss that when he popped his clogs. Summer had always been his favourite season. Well, apart from the sound of the ice-cream van. Thinking about it now, he should have got rid of that irritation yonks ago. It hadn't exactly been hard.

He crossed the street, head down, hands in his pockets, then hovered outside Mrs Robin's house. The door was closed; there was no movement in any of the windows. She'd be out the back, as was her habit, or so Tammy had told him once.

Mike studied the gnomes. The one bending over and showing his round pink arse was particularly vulgar, but it reminded Mike of how Wayne the Pain had looked when he'd left him the night before—blood staining his bed, throat slashed, and carrot poking from his bum.

Mike chuckled and opened the small metal gate. It creaked, and he frowned at the hinge. What a nuisance.

But then it only took him a second to swipe up the bum-showing gnome. He left the gate open—he'd be back—and scarpered over the street.

He let himself in, glancing up the stairs to make sure *she* hadn't escaped and was trying to get out.

She wasn't.

Mike opened the dining room door, surveyed the smash of destroyed gnomes, then threw in the one he was holding. To his disappointment, it stayed in one piece and rolled to a halt beneath the table.

It didn't really matter. He'd have a rolling pin session with the new gnomes later. Break them all up beyond recognition.

Quickly, he let himself out of his house again, closing the door, then scooting over the street.

Which one to take this time? Could he carry two? It would minimise his chance of getting caught.

Suddenly, Mrs Robin's front door opened.

She stood there, dressed in a flowery blue dress and with her tightly curled hair more unkempt than he'd ever seen it before.

"Mr Mendes," she said. "What are you doing?"

"I...er...I heard that Tammy was missing." His heart was pounding. Another second and he'd have had two gnomes beneath his arms.

"You did?" Her eyes widened. "How?"

"The...er...police. They knocked on my door. Asked if I saw anything." Well, that was the truth at least.

"And did you?" She knotted her gnarly old hands together.

"Sadly, no." He stepped up to her, fascinated suddenly by her tiny bird-like frame. It was as if she were made of the thinnest noodles and her papery skin stretched over each bone.

She'd be so easy to kill.

"Oh, that's a shame." Her wizened old face drooped. "It seems the police are at a dead end as to her whereabouts."

"You must be so worried."

"Oh, I am. Really I am. Tammy is my world, you know she is, you must notice that she's here all the time. So much more than my other children. She's my rock, I don't know what I'd do without her. Each day she brings me lunch and..."

"Yeah, I've noticed." He nodded over her shoulder. "Have you had lunch today?"

"Oh no, I couldn't eat."

"But you should."

"I haven't the energy to make anything, and eating alone it's...well, it's just too lonely."

"I agree, it is lonely." He sighed. "I hate it."

She frowned at him. "You look well. Did the chemotherapy work?"

He smiled. "The jury is still out. I tell you what, why don't I come in, make us both a sandwich or something. Take your mind off worrying about Tammy for a bit. Nothing you can do from here, and I'm sure the police are doing their best, searching the woods, rivers, and ditches as we speak."

"Oh dear." She clasped her hand to her mouth. "Woods, rivers, and ditches."

"Ah, take no notice of me. I have no idea what the police do in these cases."

"I suppose." She stepped back and sniffed. "And if you don't mind, I would appreciate some company. The mind wanders when you're on your own, you see. Goes down all kinds of strange paths, thinking the worst and wondering about what-ifs."

"Tell me about it. I spend a lot of time alone." He stepped into the house, noticing that she only came up to his shoulder and would surely only be a third of his weight, probably only a quarter when he'd been at his heaviest and fighting.

"I know that." She shut the door. "How is work going?"

"Not doing much, you know, since the diagnosis."

"I don't blame you. Being so ill gives you a wake-up call, doesn't it. Makes you realise you have to live for the day, do things that bring you pleasure. I felt like that when I had my heart attack—that was nine years ago now, mind." She walked past him into the kitchen and flicked the kettle on. "Old ticker has kept on going, though." She patted her scrawny chest.

Mike took a seat at the pine table, leaned back, and crossed his ankles. This was fun, watching her move about. It gave him ideas about how to kill her. Should he snap her neck like the pharmacist? No, he'd done that. What about cutting her throat? No, done that, too. He'd always fancied seeing what was inside a human's abdomen, close up. All those sausage strings of intestines, the delicate kidneys that were so easy to target with a punch. The diaphragm skirt, the shiny liver, the temperamental pancreas that in his case had waved a sign 'Cancer Welcome Here'.

Mmm, perhaps that was what he'd do. Gut her alive and explore her innards. The last sights she'd see would be of him taking them from her abdominal cavity, holding them up while they were warm and beating in his hands.

"Tea or coffee?" she asked.

"Tea, please." He tipped his head and wondered where she kept her knives. Unlike Wayne the Pain, she didn't have them on show.

She clattered in a cupboard then withdrew a loaf of bread. "This is still fresh; would you like ham or cheese?"

"I'm supposed to be making you lunch," he said, placing his hands behind his head, elbows out to the side.

"Oh, don't worry, I know the way around my own kitchen. And perhaps the act of making food for two will give me an appetite." She paused and looked at the windowsill.

Mike followed her line of sight. On it sat a photograph, in a silver frame, of Tammy. She wore her usual low top, big boobs pressed together to make a sweet cleavage he'd become fond of using. A necklace with a strawberry sat above it, the same colour as her bright lipstick. Her lashes were long and fluttery, the way they had been when he'd taken her—not that they were like that now, they'd become all smudged and cakey, a bit gross really.

"Oh, my poor sweet girl," Mrs Robin said with a shaky voice. "Where are you?"

"Cheese," Mike said.

"What?" She spun to face him.

"Cheese, in my sandwich. If that's okay."

"Oh, er, yes, of course." She went to the fridge and produced a chunk of cheddar. "Piccalilli?"

"Even better."

She managed a weak smile and turned to the breadboard.

Mike lowered his arms and stood. He felt big, huge, a powerful strength in this small house with this small, pathetically weak old woman.

He breathed deep, filling his lungs to the maximum, and closed his eyes, relishing the life-force and energy within. It wouldn't be there for much longer, but while it was, he'd appreciate it, revel in it.

Mrs Robin leaned to the right and opened a drawer. She plucked a butter knife from it but left it open.

The kettle came to the boil, rumbling as steam poured from the spout.

Mike licked his dry lips and studied the contents of the drawer.

Perfect.

There were several sharp knives, ideal for gutting, and a pair of scissors, maybe he'd need them, too.

"Tammy made the piccalilli," Mrs Robin said.

"Did she?"

"Yes, she's a clever girl, a real whizz in the kitchen."

She is in the bedroom, too.

He reached into his pocket and withdrew a thin pair of latex gloves. He hadn't actually touched anything yet, had been careful not to. But that was about to change.

The knives were calling him.

So was the need to cut into Mrs Robin. Tick off another all-important thing on his list and find out what was inside her, how she'd look with the contents of her torso spilling onto her kitchen floor.

"It's yesterday's bread, but it's still soft," she said, digging into the piccalilli jar. "I don't mind it for a few days, I'm not the fussy sort."

The vegetable knife was short and sharp—it cut into a neck well, Mike knew that from experience. The carving knife might be better for this, though, to really get deep. Or should he use the one in between, with a thick silver blade.

Yes, that one would do, it was even twinkling at him. Inviting him to pick it up.

He reached into the drawer, curled his fingers around the knife handle, and grinned.

Show time.

Ding dong.

"Oh, that might be the police with news on Tammy." Mrs Robin clattered the knife she was holding to the breadboard and rushed past Mike, travelling faster than he'd thought someone of her age could.

Mike released the blade and stepped back. He whisked off the gloves and shoved them into his pocket and held them there in his fists.

"Ah, it is you." Mrs Robin's voice filtered into the kitchen. "Have you found her? Have you found my Tammy?"

Mike frowned. Of course they hadn't found her, and they wouldn't if he could help it—at least not until they were both dead.

But what a bloody inconvenient time for them to show up. Just when Mike was about to have some fun and make the most of his day as Doctor Linnel had told him to.

Chapter Twelve

Shona and Earle had waited three minutes at Mike Mendes' door. He'd been home the day before at this time, though today there was no TV flickering on the other side of the yellowing nets.

Eventually, they'd given up and walked back down his narrow garden path.

"And now," Shona said, gesturing to Mrs Robin's house. "We should tell Mrs Robin that we've found Tammy's car in Ealing Woods. It would be better coming from us rather than uniform."

"Yeah, I agree." Earle nodded and opened the low squeaky gate to Mrs Robin's front garden. "She might have remembered something of use, too."

"It's weird, a missing person and two murders. The deaths are connected, we know that because of the cryptic messages in Portuguese, but..."

"But Julie thinks the black fibres found in Tammy's car and in the ice-cream van may be a match."

"And if they are, which I'm guessing they will be, why have we found two bodies and not three?"

"Perhaps we just haven't found Tammy's yet."

Shona's heart sank. That was the last thing she wanted to find.

"There is another possibility, though," Earle said.

"What's that?"

"She isn't dead, she's being kept alive somewhere by this sicko. The other victims are men, after all. Maybe he likes women warm."

A shudder tapped its way up her spine as she rang Mrs Robin's doorbell. "I must admit, that's crossed my mind as well."

"Which means we have to find her ASAP, we know what he's capable of. When he's finished, had his fun, he'll slit her throat or something equally horrific."

"And what she must be going through, right now, at his hands defies the imagination."

The door opened. Mrs Robin appeared even frailer, her eyes more sunken and her skin ashen.

"Ah, it is you." She pressed her bony hand to her chest, and her bottom lip wobbled. "Have you found her? Have you found my Tammy?"

"No, not yet, sorry." Shona smiled. "We just wanted to let you know we've recovered Tammy's car."

"You have?"

"Could we come in?" Earle asked.

"Yes, yes, of course." She stepped back, opening the door wide. "Please, this way. The kettle has just boiled." Her voice was high-pitched, the tension in her small body seeming to constrict her throat.

Shona and Earle walked down the hallway and into the kitchen.

"Mr Mendes." Shona came to an abrupt halt when she saw the big man she'd moments ago been searching for.

"Ah, Officer." He shut the drawer he was standing next to. His gaze flicked from Shona to Earle.

"What are you doing here?" Shona forced a smile.

The bloke looked shifty, standing by the hob like that, shoving something in his pocket. A tissue?

"I came to see Mrs Robin. See if there was anything I could do to help, what with Tammy being missing." He paused. "Just trying to be a good neighbour and all that."

"Do you know Tammy?" Shona asked.

"No, you don't, do you," Mrs Robin said, flicking the kettle on.

"Well, we've said hello, passed the time of day on occasion," Mike said with a shrug and stared down at his black boots.

"You have?" Mrs Robin raised her eyebrows at him. "Tammy didn't say."

"Yeah, she's...well, she's on the street a lot, isn't she." He fidgeted from one foot to the other. "We bump into each other."

"But you don't recall seeing her leave here on Monday?" Shona asked again.

"Nope, sorry." Another shrug.

"Here, have your sarnie." Mrs Robin handed him a plate with a skinny cheese sandwich on it. A blob of neon-yellow chutney oozed from the crust.

He took it. "I'm not that hungry anymore. Should probably go."

"Oh, but I made it especially."

He set it on the table and scratched his head.

"Please, don't let us interrupt your lunch." Shona gestured to the chair set at an angle to the table. Someone had sat in it but not pushed it back in when they'd stood. She guessed it had been Mike.

He hesitated for a second then sat. The bloke was big—despite him having said he had cancer, there was some strength to him.

He saw her studying him. "I stopped chemo a while ago, it wasn't doing anything, and the sickness was torture. So I'm eating everything and anything while I can, while my body is letting me. Won't last long, the doc tells me a few months at best." He rubbed his right side, over his liver.

"I really am sorry," Shona said. "Are you in pain?"

"It comes and goes." He bit into the sandwich, chewed, then swallowed. "I'm okay if I've got some codeine, will probably need something stronger at the end."

"Oh, Mike, you really are so brave to talk about it like this." Mrs Robin shook her head. Her eyes were misting.

"It's a fact." He slurped on his tea, "nothing I can do about it but respect the life I have left."

Shona frowned; she'd heard that before recently. Hadn't she?

"God bless you." Mrs Robin wiped her fingers on a tea towel. She was quiet for a few seconds, then, "You said you recovered Tammy's car, Officer." She gulped, as though wanting, but not wanting more information.

"Yes, we did. In Ealing Woods," Shona said.

Mike coughed. It was a real chest-shaking, rib-rattling choke, and he walloped his sternum.

"Are you okay, sir?" Earle asked.

He quieted, cleared his throat. "Er...yes, went down the wrong way, that's all." He pulled in a deep breath.

Shona returned her attention to Mrs Robin. "Is there any reason your daughter would go there?"

"No, oh no, not at all." Mrs Robin paled. "The woods, no, why would she? And on her own..."

"Here, sit down." Earle dragged out the other chair, and Shona steered Mrs Robin to it.

She sat, wafting her hand in front of her face. "I'm so worried, I really am. I can't sleep, can't eat, that's why Mike is here having lunch with me, and...oh dear..."

"We're doing everything we can," Shona said. "We've got our forensic team analysing the car as we speak."

"You have?" Mrs Robin said.

"Yes."

"Have they found anything? Any clues?" She appeared hopeful.

"We may have found something to link her to another case." Shona glanced at Mike.

He'd set down his half-eaten sandwich and was staring at her with his lips parted, unblinking. He looked gormless with crumbs in the corner of his mouth, and those cat scratches on his cheek didn't help.

"Another case?" Mrs Robin repeated.

"Does Tammy know the ice-cream man, the regular one who comes around the estate?" Shona asked.

Mike poked at his pocket. There was something soft in there. A handkerchief perhaps.

"Well, I...no, not that I know of. I mean, on the odd occasion she's gone out to get us a ninety-nine each, when the weather was balmy, but I wouldn't say she knows him, why?"

Shona glanced at Earle.

"He's been the victim of a crime," Earle said.

"A murder," Shona added. "And evidence from where he was killed and evidence in Tammy's car appear to match."

"What? What did you find?" Mike snapped.

Shona raised her eyebrows at him. Did he have a thing for Tammy? A crush? Was that why he was really here? Not that Shona could imagine Tammy going for Mike. He wasn't totally ugly, but there was something a bit odd going on with him, as if he didn't quite hit the spot socially. Awkward, that was what he was.

The poor bloke is dying, Shona, give him a break.

"Fabric fibres," she said, "that's all I can say for now, but I'm pretty sure Tammy didn't drive the car to the woods. A camera picked up an image—the person in the driver's seat appears bigger, broader than her."

"So where is she?" Mrs Robin asked, standing then sitting back down with a bump. "You have to find her."

"We'll do our best." Shona rested her hand on Mrs Robin's arm. "We really will." Her phone rang. Darren.

"Hey." She pressed it to her ear.

"You're not going to like this, ma'am."

"Bloody hell," she muttered, turning away from the table. "Now what?"

"Body in a wheelie bin. Appears to have had his neck broken."

"Neck broken. Jesus, when will this end?" She paused and turned to Earle, raised her eyebrows.

He sighed, having heard enough of the conversation to know their day was going downhill rapidly.

"Send me the address, we'll get there ASAP. And make sure SOCO are on their way, too. And I know they're busy, but needs must."

"Yes, ma'am."

She hung up. "I'm sorry, Mrs Robin, we have to go."

"Is it Tammy?" She twisted her hands together.

"No, no, it isn't."

"What then?" Mike stood, the chair legs scraping on the hard tiled floor. "What is it? Where are you going?"

She looked up and up some more. He loomed over her, and she didn't like it. He was easily as tall as Earle, but the glint in his eye sent a slither of unease over her skin. "Another case, Mr Mendes."

"A broken neck?" he said.

"Pardon?"

"You said neck broken on the phone."

"Er, did I?" What was he implying? What did he want her to say? Was he one of those oddballs who enjoyed all the gruesome details of real-life crime? "Actually, Mr Mendes, while I have you here…"

He swallowed and once again tugged at the dry skin on his lips with his top teeth. He glanced at the door to the hallway.

"I was in the property behind yours earlier," Shona said, "upstairs, and I noticed that you have a back window that has a view over both gardens."

"What?"

"Your upstairs window, near the big tree, the one the cat was stuck in, I presume." She pointed at his scabbing scratches.

"Oh, er, yes."

"The curtains were closed, or is it a blind, and—"

"So." He folded his arms, his knuckles pressing on his black jumper and creasing it. "So what if the blind was closed? Not a crime, is it?"

"It doesn't matter at all, I just wondered if when you opened it, or closed it last, you saw anything suspicious going on in the house behind."

"I keep it closed, don't use that room."

"Oh, that's a shame."

"So I haven't seen anything from that window. Nothing at all."

"Are you sure?"

"Yeah. Why?"

She tilted her head and watched a small muscle jump over and over in his cheek. "We are investigating several cases in the area, Mr Mendes, so as you can imagine, witnesses are vital to us." She withdrew a card. "If you see anything or remember anything about Tammy, or the property behind yours, please call me."

He took it in his big fingers. "Yeah, I will, but I doubt anything will come to me." He tapped his head. "Got cancer in here, too, or so they told me."

"Oh, Mike." Mrs Robin tutted. "You poor, poor thing. I wish there was more I could do to help you. I'll pray for you, every day."

****

Mike was sure the stupid, vinegary cheese sandwich was going to show itself again as he rushed over the street and into his home. He chained and locked the door with a clatter, then rushed around checking each room was the same as when he'd left it.

Yeah, it was. The dining room awash with smashed gnomes, and the kitchen spick and span. There was no sign of the bloody cat in the back garden, though he saw movement in Wayne the Pain's bedroom. Likely they were removing the body. Wouldn't be long till Wayne was buried, food for the worms. Mike would see him in Hell.

He left the box room until last to check, and was pleased to find she hadn't pissed herself again—because that was just bloody annoying, and if he were honest, inconsiderate. He shoved his trousers off and set about releasing the gnawing tension his interaction with the police had built in him. It was as if their voices and their penetrating stares had wound every muscle and tendon in his body up into small springs. He threw all of his energy into his fun, swallowing the taste of the piccalilli when he thrust as though it was the last fuck of his life.

Spent, he rolled off and staggered to the shower. He needed another codeine. All this expulsion of energy and the stress of having the police breathing down his neck wasn't helping his physical condition. In fact, it seemed to be sending him downwards faster.

It was *her* fault. Bitch. Making him want her all the time. She was sucking the life from him.

Perhaps he'd have to kill her sooner than planned. Have a final day of fun then off her. He could chop her up on the kitchen table, then hide her in the freezer in little plastic bags and Tupperware pots. No one would find her until he'd gone up in smoke at the crematorium, and then it would be some poor fucker who came to empty his house. Mike chuckled and poured himself a generous single malt. Likely they'd think they'd found some tasty chops, or a few prime joints. It would be hysterical if they sneaked them home and cooked Tammy up as a Sunday dinner for all the family to enjoy.

He knocked back the whisky, enjoying the heat on the back of his tongue. He poured another.

Yeah, he'd have to kill her. She'd left him no choice. Ironash was beginning to make him itch, and it was time to leave. He'd bring forward his bucket list plans and get himself to Portishead as soon as. There was bound to be an Airbnb he could get for a few months, plonk the expense on his credit card. He'd get somewhere with a view, order what he wanted from Amazon and the grocery store, and maybe…

He walked to the window, yanked back the net, and looked out. The young mother from the end of the road was strolling past pushing a double buggy.

…maybe he'd get himself another woman in Portishead. If he got a detached property with a spare room, that could work. He grinned and watched the woman go from view. He liked her hair, it was long and dark. He'd bet it smelled delicious.

Chapter Thirteen

Earle parked at the front of the parade of shops on Cory. The side alley was cordoned off, and two uniforms stood there chatting.

"Did you think…?" Shona said.

"What?"

She undid her seat belt but made no move to get out of the car.

"What?" Earle asked again.

"I feel like a right cold-hearted bitch for saying this, but did you think Mike Mendes was a bit odd?"

"Why does that make you feel like a bitch?"

"Well, he's dying, isn't he. Cancer."

"He didn't look too bad to me, not how I'd imagine someone with cancer to look anyway."

"Mmm, he said his appetite was back after chemotherapy and he was eating everything." She tapped her fingers together. "There's just something I can't put my finger on."

"Like what?"

"He's a bit…shifty. He seemed uncomfortable with us being there."

"With police being there. He wouldn't be the first. Doesn't necessarily mean anything." He paused. "He was more jittery than I'd expect, though, and interested in our next case."

"I know, right." She paused, her belly tightening the way it did when it was trying to get her to listen. "But if he'd only just called in to Mrs Robin to be neighbourly, what's he got to hide or be shifty about?" She remembered how he'd been lurking in the kitchen when she'd arrived rather than sitting waiting for his host to return from the front door. "And why didn't he see Tammy leave, or her car leave? If he was home, which he said he was, his living room is right there, opposite."

"He could have been in the kitchen or the bathroom."

"True." But Shona's guts didn't believe that, and she'd learnt over time to believe her guts. "I might just run a check on him."

"Mike Mendes?" Earle raised his eyebrows. "You think he could have something to do with it?"

"What colour fibres had Julie collected from the car and the van?"

"Black." He nodded slowly. "And he was wearing a black jumper, I noticed. It's a warm day, seemed odd."

"Which I can't get him in for, hardly a crime…but…" She plucked her phone from her pocket and tapped the screen. "Andy, you busy?"

"Not as busy as Darren. A bunch of eight teenagers got caught nicking stuff from Superdrug, and the manager is insisting they're all charged. It's chaos down there in reception, and all for a few lipsticks and Lynx."

"Wow, I'm glad I rang you and not him."

"Well, I am your tech guy. What do you want?" There was a note of irritation in his voice.

She smiled. "Can you run a check on a Mike Mendes for me? He lives opposite Tammy Robin's mother."

"The missing woman."

"Yes."

"Anything specific?"

"No, not really. Just has he got a record, employment, that kind of thing."

"On it."

"Thanks."

"Oh, and that other guy, nickname Badger," Andy said. "While I have you on the line, ma'am."

"Yes?"

"He told the parole board that his post prison address would be London. Apparently he has family there."

"Oh, okay, thanks. I appreciate it."

"Anything else I can do for you, ma'am?"

"No, I think that's it."

"No one else in Ironash you want me to look into?"

"Er, no."

"Male?"

"No."

"Sure?"

"Yes, I'm sure." She frowned. Was he nudging her to do a search on Ben the way Earle had? "Speak later, Andy." She put her phone away. What was it with these blokes? Protective much? "Badger is in London apparently."

"He is?" Earle raised his eyebrows. "For definite?"

"According to his parole records."

He pursed his lips and blew out a breath. "Good, let's hope he stays there."

"Earle..."

"Mmm?" He pulled the handle on his door, and it clicked open an inch. "What?"

"If he's in London, why would Patrick tell you to watch your back? And why would he be so sure Badger was involved in *his* shooting in Manchester?"

"I don't know." Earle frowned.

"I think you should call him."

"Patrick?"

"Yes."

"She wouldn't like that."

"Who?"

"Fiona." He rubbed his fingers over his brow, as though trying to smooth away the frown lines there. "Fiona wouldn't like that one bit."

"Why not?" What the heck had happened that meant Earle and his ex-partner could have no contact? What could be so bad? "What went on between you all?" She braced for a sharp response.

He sighed. "I don't want to talk about it."

"I respect that, really I do. But I care, and because I care, we need all the facts, we need to know why Patrick thinks it was Badger who shot him." She placed her hand on Earle's arm. "I don't like the thought of someone out there wanting vengeance on you."

He swallowed and nodded slowly. "I don't like that thought either. Gives me the chills, to be honest." He turned to her. "You're right. I'll call Patrick."

"You will?"

"Yeah, once we've dealt with this shitstorm and found Tammy. She has to be our priority."

She smiled. "Come on, let's check this scene out. We can't help the poor bugger who's had his neck broken, but there might be a clue as to where she is."

"I hope so, because I have a horrible feeling we're running out of time."

"I agree, this bastard isn't hanging around. Three kills in as many days." She paused. "It's as if he's cramming it in."

"Yeah, like *he's* running out of time."

They walked up to the uniforms, signed the log, then grabbed protectives from a box.

"Is SOCO here?" Shona asked one of the uniforms.

"Yes, ma'am, Julie Summers. Van is round the back."

"Good, thanks." They headed around the rear of the building. "That'll give us a chance to touch base with her about the fibres."

The scene before them wasn't pretty. A huge wheelie bin had been emptied onto its side. Several officers dressed in white protective gear were on their hands and knees sifting through the ripped black bags and their stinky contents. To the right of them, a body had been laid out, and Julie was crouched next to it, face mask on.

When she spotted them, she stood and drew down her mask. "Hey, you two."

"We meet again." Earle sighed.

"Maybe we should all grab a drink at Grapes Ahoy at the weekend, have a chat that isn't over a corpse." Julie smiled.

"Good idea, Julie," Shona said. "Any idea who this is?"

"Yes, one Rufus Drake according to his driving licence. Lives in Overbridge, fifty-five years old."

Earle retrieved his phone. "Want me to get Andy on it, Shona?"

"Please."

He stepped away, phone pressed to his ear.

"Death by..." Shona said, tipping her head and studying the body. "Not that I really need to ask."

"There's always more to a body than meets the eye." Julie hovered her finger over the neck. "Broken."

"I can see that."

The victim's head was stretched to the right in a sickeningly unnatural angle—his chin pointing upwards, tendons taut and Adam's apple jutting sideways. He had a fancy moustache, which was remarkably neat considering the circumstances. His eyes were half closed, mouth trapped in what appeared to be a cry.

"He's not a very big bloke," Shona said. "Can't imagine he'd put up much of a fight if someone was intent on doing him harm."

"Which they obviously were."

"Mmm." She looked at his hands. There was no evidence of bruising or swelling. He hadn't thrown any hard punches lately. "Anything beneath the nails?"

"I haven't checked yet, not been here long myself."

"How was he found, do you know?"

"Rubbish truck men. When they opened the lid to attach the wheelie bin to the truck. He was staring up at them."

"Nice."

"He vomited, the bloke who found him, which didn't help with my scene."

Shona wrinkled her nose. "Did whoever do this really think the body would just get taken away with the rubbish? Dumped in landfill?"

"Must have."

Earle stepped up, slipping his phone away. "The deceased is a pharmacist, works in this parade here. Has done for over ten years. Next of kin a daughter, lives in Spain. I've organised for her to be informed."

"Thanks," Shona said.

"Who would want to kill a pharmacist?" Julie asked.

Shona frowned. "I don't know...someone who didn't get the medication they needed maybe."

"You'd have to be pretty desperate." Julie squatted again and with gloved hands raised the victim's wrist.

"And what would do that to someone? Mental illness?" Shona was thinking out loud.

"Or pain," Earle said. "That makes people desperate."

"True." Julie lifted the deceased's hand and studied the tip of the index finger. "I'd say he was a Type 1 diabetic."

"You would?" Shona said. "How do you know that?"

"His fingertips are scarred from repeated skin breakage, the kind of tiny pricks to draw a drop of blood for a glucometer. You know, to check blood sugar. I'd say he's been doing this to his fingers for years."

"Type 1 needs to eat regularly, right?" Shona said.

"Yes, it's the more serious, the type that means you need a good routine of eating and exercise and working out the right insulin dose."

"So..." Shona glanced around. A small red car sat alone. "So he left work...when, do you think?"

"This body is more than twelve hours old but less than twenty-four hour." Julie set his hand down. "Rigor has been and gone."

"So that time frame would work if we presume he left work yesterday evening when the pharmacy shut, likely to go home and eat to keep his blood sugar stable, and then..."

Earle nodded. "Sounds about right to me."

"And then..." Shona shook her head, her thoughts connecting. "Someone offed him when he got back here, to his car, but why? Because they were off their meds and schizophrenic, crazed maybe? Because they were in pain, discomfort, sick, and he didn't give them what they needed? Could rage do that? Does that make any sense?"

"Not to us," Earle said, "but we wouldn't go around breaking people's necks if they didn't fill a prescription."

"Jesus." Shona yanked her hair band out, her scalp suddenly tight. What a senseless death. What a waste of a life.

Just like all the rest.

"We need to find out who his last customers were," she said, dragging her hair up again and flicking the band into place.

Earle glanced at his phone. "I had Andy check to see if there is any CCTV around here."

"And?"

"There is." Earle shrugged. "But it's broken, due for repair next week."

"Well, that's no bloody good."

"There might be some in the pharmacy," Julie offered.

"Good thinking." Shona nodded at Julie. "We'll go and check that out. See if there were any other staff working with him at closing time yesterday. Oh, and any news on the fibres from Miss Robin's car and the ice-cream van?"

"They're a definite match," Julie said. "Black wool blend, pretty common, though. And also the car seat was pushed back as far as it would go. How tall is the female you're looking for?"

"Without heels, I'm guessing not very," Earle said. "Fraction taller than DI Williams here."

"So someone big *was* driving it when it was caught on camera." That made sense to Shona but wasn't much help at this stage. All it proved was that her car was dumped, which they'd deduced anyway.

"You met Kyle McFarlane yet?" Julie asked.

"Your new SOCO bloke, yes, seems nice enough," Shona said.

"He's moved here, doesn't know anyone, but I'm glad he has jumped on board, I've certainly got the work for him." Julie sighed. "Unfortunately."

"We appreciate everything you're doing."

"Cheers for that." She pointed at the car. "You might want to check that out before you go, there's another cryptic message."

"What!" Shona's heart skipped. "Like on the ice-cream van?"

"Yes, in Portuguese."

"What does it say?"

"I haven't had chance to translate it."

Shona and Earle rushed to the Fiesta.

"I'm guessing this was Rufus's car," Earle said.

"I'd say so."

The driver's door was open. On the seat was a slip of paper.

A vida é curta viva.

Shona copied it into the translation app on her phone.

"Life is short, live it." She looked up at Earle. "What the hell does that mean?"

"The murderer certainly made life short for his victims."

"What did the other notes say?"

"The first one..." Earle flipped his notebook open. "Revenge is sweet, that was on the ice-cream van."

"So the ice-cream man, Barry White, did something to annoy the killer and he was getting revenge. Like what, though? What did he do that was so irritating?"

"The music can be bloody annoying."

"Murder annoying?"

Earle said nothing.

"You're right, we have no idea what spurs people into killing. What did the second one say again, at Wayne Farthing's place?"

"That was: respect life, respect each other."

"But the bloke, and I'm guessing it's a man here, has no respect for life." She pulled out her lip balm and applied it, feeling the frown etching between her eyebrows. "Mike Mendes said something about respecting the life he had left, earlier, do you remember?"

"Yeah, I think so." Earle paused. "But why Portuguese? Mendes is as Brit as they come."

"I agree, but he was wearing a black jumper, remember."

"And he does live behind one of the murder victims and opposite Tammy."

"Enough to bring him in?" Even as she said it, she knew they couldn't. "I wonder what he did for a job, before he got ill."

"Why don't you call Andy, ask him what he's found so far."

"That's a good idea." She plucked out her phone. "Sorry to hassle you on this, Andy, and it's nothing more than an itch I can't stop worrying at, about Mike Mendes."

"I've just finished digging into him, was just about to call you."

"Go for it."

"Born and raised in Ironash, no mention of a father, and his mother ran out on him. He was on Social Services' radar for a while, back in the seventies, but was then placed in the care of his grandmother, a Mariana Mendes."

"Unusual name."

"Foreign, I think. He went to Dale High, left at sixteen, and from what I can tell flitted around job wise. I'm guessing when his grandmother died he inherited the house so never had the worry of keeping a roof over his head. Seems his main thing was boxing, did reasonably well in amateur heavyweight."

"I can see that, he's pretty big. Any previous?"

"Only one thing to mention—he was found not guilty of dangerous driving, five years ago after a crash involving a woman and her three children. All killed."

"Shit, that's terrible."

"I know. They've made some alterations to that junction now."

Shona closed her eyes and drew in a deep breath. What a horrific thing to happen, for all involved.

"Thanks, Andy. Appreciate it."

"No problem, oh, and one other thing."

"What?"

"I Googled him."

"Who?" If he said Ben Thomas, she'd loose her shit.

"Mike Mendes."

"Oh, okay, and..." She stepped away from the car, and her attention settled on Julie directing a police photographer.

"Seems he runs a small business from home."

"Doing what?"

"A website came up, offering translation services."

"Translation? What, like switching things from one language to another?" Her heart rate picked up. She spun to Earle and held up her right index finger.

He stiffened, clearly sensing something was coming, and studied her face.

"Yeah," Andy went on, "he offers an online service translating English to Portuguese and vice versa. I'm guessing that's where his grandmother's unusual first name is from, Portugal."

"Portuguese." Her mind was sparking, thoughts and connections lighting up her brain. Adrenaline shot into her veins. "Portuguese. Oh my God, Andy, thank you. That's perfect."

"It is?"

"Yes, can't explain now." She hung up and stared at Earle. "Mike Mendes is fluent in Portuguese."

"No way."

"Yes way. And how many other people in Ironash speak that language?"

"I've never come across anyone. And with these notes left at the scenes..."

"We need to get round there, fast."

"Bloody hell, we do. And you were right to think he was shifty. He really fucking is."

Chapter Fourteen

Earle put his foot to the floor as they raced back to the Whilton Estate. Shona dialled into their DCI to bring him up to speed.

"We're going back to see a Mike Mendes," Shona told Fletcher.

"What do you have on him?" Fletcher asked.

"Circumstantial at the moment, but definitely worth a talking to."

"Okay. You think the murders are connected, right?"

"Yes, and the killer wants us to know that, hence the notes."

"And the missing woman?"

"Connected to the murders, we think."

"And why is this Mendes fella a red flag?"

"Fibres in Miss Robin's car and the ice-cream van could be a match to a jumper we've actually seen him wearing. Plus he's in the right location. By that I mean, walking distance to all of the crime scenes, and he's a Portuguese speaker."

"What does that have to do with it?"

"The notes left at the murder sites are in Portuguese."

"Oh, well, yes, you do need to speak to him."

"He has cancer, sir, not long to live apparently."

"That's no excuse to take innocent souls with him."

"I agree."

"Keep me up to date."

"I will, sir." Shona ended the call.

Earl parked up outside Mike's house. The net curtain twitched.

"He's in," she said, reaching for a pair of cuffs from the glove compartment and sliding them into her jacket pocket. "Best make sure he doesn't make a run for it."

"Do you think we should call for backup?"

She hesitated. Tried to listen to her gut. "You know what, I don't think that would hurt."

"Good call." Earle drew out his phone and had a brief conversation with Darren.

"Come on, and keep your wits about you." She opened the car door. "If he's guilty of three murders, he's really bloody dangerous, plus prison isn't going to mean much to him if he's on his last months of life."

"If he is guilty then I'm glad he's going to meet his maker soon and be judged for it."

Shona climbed out. "Circumstantial at the moment, remember."

They walked up to the front door. Earle rang the bell. He had to do it twice before Mike opened it a crack.

"What do you want?" he asked with a frown. His wispy hair was dishevelled, and he had a spot of piccalilli between his front teeth.

"Mr Mendes, hello again. I wonder if we could come in and ask you a few questions," Shona said.

"It's not convenient," he snapped, starting to shut the door.

She whacked her palm on it. "It won't take long."

"I've told you, I didn't see Tammy the other day, or since, or her car." He glanced over his shoulder. "I have nothing to add to that."

"And we appreciate the information, but there's a few other things we'd like to discuss with you."

"Like what?" He was rattling the chain. The noise was annoying.

"As I mentioned, there's been a murder in the house directly behind yours. We are doing routine calls to everyone along this side of the street."

"You are?"

He'd removed the black jumper and now wore a white t-shirt with a small frayed rip in the neck and a blue Nike hoody.

"Yes." She smiled and nodded at the door. "So can we go into your back garden and see if there is any evidence?"

"There isn't."

"Have you looked?"

"Er...?"

"I'll take that as a no, Mr Mendes. Now, if you don't mind, just a few minutes, then we'll be on our way."

He tensed his jaw, his dry lips cracking together.

Shona held his eye contact. His pupils were wide black holes, and she was sure they were hiding something in their depths. She just didn't know what but had a feeling it was a dark secret, something he didn't want her to nosey at.

"Mr Mendes," Earle said, his voice extra deep as he puffed up his broad chest and tilted his chin. "Your cooperation would be very much appreciated."

Mike glanced at him with now narrowed eyes then held the door wide. "Okay, but I'm busy, working, so just for a few minutes."

"Thank you." Shona stepped past him. "I'm surprised you're working. The other day you said you didn't anymore, because of your illness."

"Oh, well…I have to tie up a few loose ends, you know, before I kick the bucket." He ushered them along the hallway and past the banister. "This way."

The wooden laminate flooring had a little patch of small white crumbs beside a closed door. They seemed to be porcelain, shiny and sharp.

"Come through to the back garden." Mike spoke loud and urged them to keep moving. "Though I'm sure you'll find there's nothing to see."

Shona stopped in the centre of the kitchen. "How long are you expecting to stay at home alone with your illness?"

He frowned, and his shoulders rounded.

Was he cross that she'd stopped when he'd clearly wanted her to move through the house, or was it her question?

"As long as I can," he said with a shrug. "Never did like hospitals."

"You spent much time in them?" Earle asked.

"Not until the last six months. Got a few stitches when I was boxing, way back when, but never an overnight stay." He appeared to suppress a shudder. "Now I guess I'll end my days there."

"I'm sure you'll be very well looked after," Shona said. Her attention went behind Mike, to a magnet on the fridge. A footballer, quite handsome, dark hair. For a moment Shona rummaged through her brain to remember his name, then it came to her. Cristiano Ronaldo.

"You like football?" she asked.

"Yeah, I do. I like most sports actually." Mike opened the back door. "Shall we?"

"He's a footballer, isn't he?" Shona pointed at the magnet.

"Yeah, the best in the world, no question. Shall we…?" He gestured to the garden with a flick of his wrist.

Shona scratched the side of her head and made a show of concentrating. "I'm trying to remember his name."

"Ronaldo."

"Ah, yes, Cristiano Ronaldo. He's from Portugal, right?"

"Yeah, he is. The garden is this way."

"You ever been to Portugal, Mr Mendes? I hear it's very beautiful, especially the Algarve."

"Nope, never."

"But you can speak the language." Shona studied him, keen to see his reaction to her statement.

He stiffened. "Er, yeah."

"How? If you don't mind me asking."

"My grandmother, she was from Lisbon."

"Ah, I see." The ticks were adding up fast against Mike's name. But would he talk and did he have Tammy?

Bump.

Shona snatched a look at Earle. Had she imagined the quiet thud above them?

Earle nodded, a very small movement. He'd heard it, too.

Bloody hell. Has he got her stashed upstairs?

Surely that was too simple. They wouldn't be so lucky. But stranger things happened.

Mike balled his hands into fists. "The garden...this way..."

"Are you here alone?" Shona asked, making no move to step towards the open back door. "In the house, I mean."

Bang.

"Yeah, well, apart from the cat, you know. Jumps around. Bangs." He shrugged, and a forced smile stretched his lips. "Like that."

"It's *your* cat?"

"Er, yeah, it's mine."

"Forgive me if I'm muddled, but you said you got those scratches on your face from a neighbour's cat you were helping down from the tree." She gestured to his cheek.

He touched his face. His nostrils flared, and he glanced at the hallway and the still open front door.

The hairs on the back of Shona's neck rose, her stomach tightened, and her mouth dried. This was the calm before the storm, the split second before a tsunami wave struck land.

But she had to play it cool.

Another bang.

Then another.

Adrenaline punched into her bloodstream. No way was that a cat. Someone was up there, and if she had to put money on it, she'd say it was Tammy Robin. "Noisy cat. Big, is it?"

Will he break?

"Bloody fat thing. I'll go and get it." Mike paced from the door, brow creased, arms swinging. "Should stop feeding it really, for a while at least."

Shona stepped in front of him and found herself having to look up. "DS Montague can get the cat."

"What? No." Panic ran riot over Mike's features, and his eyes widened. A sheen of sweat glowed over his top lip.

He tried to step around Shona.

Again she blocked his way. To get past her he'd have to physically move her. "Go, Earle poor thing might be stuck in a cupboard or something."

"You sure?"

"Yes."

Earle left the room.

"I can get it," Mike snapped, his cheeks blooming to scarlet. He shifted his weight from one foot to the other. "You have no right to go upstairs, this is my house, these are my things. You need a warrant to do that. This is an invasion of my privacy and my human rights. I'll, I'll..." A tremble started in his lower arms then rattled up to his biceps then shoulders. He gritted his teeth, and the tendons in his neck strained.

Shona backed up. She'd seen that action before. He was a viper coiling for attack.

For a moment, Mike stared at the empty doorway Earle had just gone through, then he turned away and rested his hands on the kitchen work surface. He hung his head, his back bowed. Some of the wound tight tension seemed to release, but only a fraction, as he blew out a breath.

"Mr Mendes?" she said as calmly as possible.

"You shouldn't have come in, any of you."

"Any of us?"

"No, none of you. Busybody police and *her*."

"Who is *her*?"

Mike turned. A flash glinted off something he was holding.

Knife.

Shit.

Shona pushed a chair beneath a table, making room to widen her stance. Mike was big, clearly capable and guilty of what they suspected he'd done, and now desperate and reckless added to the equation.

Could there be a more dangerous man?

Her heart rate shot to a gallop. Despite hearing noises upstairs—bumps, voices, scrapes, and clatters—she kept her entire focus on the vegetable knife hovering only a few feet away from her face. "Put that down, Mr Mendes."

"Why should I?" A string of spittle flew from his mouth.

"Threatening a police officer is a very serious offence."

"I've committed worse." He took a step closer. Now one long-paced lunge, and he'd be able to stick her.

I've trained for years so I'm ready for this, this exactly.

Fuck, he's big.

She swallowed, her throat tight as she tried to keep her limbs loose, ready to fly in any direction to protect herself. "What have you done, Mike?" she asked. "What do you mean by you've 'done worse'?"

Where the hell is backup?

"I've killed, that's what."

Jesus Christ. "Who have you killed?"

"*Her?*"

"Tammy Robin?"

Please no, not sweet Tammy.

Mike chuckled, a strange manic sound. "No, not that one, haven't had the chance. *Her*, I killed *her* years ago, in Ealing Woods, not far from Tammy's car if you want to dig her up when I'm six feet under."

"Who?" What was he talking about? "Who is buried in Ealing Woods?"

"Dunno really." Mike shrugged and waved the knife from left to right in a ticktock motion. "Just came across her. It was like the universe had sent me a gift. Here you go, Mikey-boy, have some fun with this one. Never really saw anything on the news, no one asked around. Never found out her name. I guess she wasn't missed."

"I don't understand." And she didn't really want to.

"Sure you do. A pretty woman like you knows what men want." He paused and licked his lips. "And that's what I took from *her*. Had to...you know..." With his free hand he drew a line over his neck. "Finish her off afterwards, wouldn't have done to get caught and go to prison. I was fighting well back then, didn't want my best years spent behind bars when I could be in the ring."

"So you raped and murdered a woman in the woods then buried the body, a long time ago?"

"Sharp, aren't you." He cackled.

Damn it, what was Earle doing? It sounded like he was dismantling a bed frame.

"And Tammy Robin? Is she upstairs?"

"Yeah." He grinned. "But I've had my fun. She's fucked up now, disgusting really."

Shona had to swallow a burn of bile that rushed up her gullet. This man was evil to the bone.

"What have you done to her?" She slipped a step to the left, towards the door and the hallway. With a bit of luck she'd have a few uniforms on her side soon.

Mike followed her, the knife making small slices through the air.

He's going to use it.

He can try.

Shona homed her senses in on Mendes, picking up all of his small movements, his breaths, each flick of his eyes which were burning bright with madness.

"How about Barry White?" Perhaps she could keep him talking until backup arrived or Earle reappeared.

"Who?" Mike frowned.

"The ice-cream man. His name was Barry White."

"Stupid fucking name, but then he was a stupid fucking man, always driving that annoying van down here, disturbing the peace, polluting the air."

"Is that why you killed him? Because he made a noise?"

"Yeah, and killing him for revenge was sweet." He laughed. "Get it? Sweet, like ice cream."

Shona didn't respond despite the well of hate for Mike Mendes that was swelling inside her. Some criminals were bad, some mad. This one, he was garden variety nasty but bloody daring with it.

"Put the knife down, Mr Mendes."

"No." He snarled, his lips peeling back.

Shona briefly considered making a dash for it, but flight wasn't an option. Mendes had long legs and would take one step to her two. She'd have to stay and fight. Turning her back on him would be a like jumping from a plane without a parachute—only one outcome. "What about Wayne Farthing? What did he do?" She'd try and buy some time. "The man who lived behind you?"

"Ah, Wayne the Pain, disrespected me, he did. Always letting his cat shit in my veg patch. And when I asked him to make it stop, he told me to fuck off."

"So you murdered him?"

"How would you like crap in your lettuce?"

She didn't answer.

"Not much, I don't think, so yeah, I bopped him off, left him with a carrot top on show, did you see that?"

She swallowed. The metallic taste of anger was filling her mouth. "And the pharmacist. A man who helped sick people for a living."

"Huh, he didn't help me. Bastard."

There were more noises upstairs, different now, footsteps.

"What did he do, or not do?" Shona asked. Mendes would strike soon, when Earle appeared. And he'd go high, she was sure of that.

Shona blocked it, leaping backwards and hitting the wall. "Mike Mendes, I'm arresting you for..." She gritted her teeth and ducked to avoid his next crack at knifing her.

This time she managed to scoot around him.

He stumbled forward, his turn to hit the wall. Before he straightened, Shona harnessed her power, gathering it from her feet, dragging it up, to her thighs, her hips, and then swinging her full body weight at the exact spot he'd been rubbing when he'd said he was in pain. Her knuckles collided with his torso; they seemed to keep on going, inwards, shoving him back to the wall.

He cried out. A real agonised, high-pitched yelp, and then doubled over.

She whacked him again, because the evil bastard had really annoyed her.

Another yelp, and the knife fell to the floor.

Quickly, she kicked it away, down the hall.

It slid to a stop beside Earle. He trapped it beneath his left boot. "Need a hand, ma'am?"

"Nope... I've got it." She whipped the cuffs from her pocket and threw herself on top of Mendes who was sprawled on the floor, groaning, eyes closed and clutching his side. "Mike Mendes." She dragged his hands together in the small of his back. "I'm arresting you..."

He groaned as his cheek bunched on the laminate and he tried and failed to curl into a ball.

"...for the murders of Barry White, Wayne Farthing, and Rufus Drake," she said breathlessly as she dumped her weight on his arse to keep him down. Not that it seemed like he could go anywhere or would even try. "You do not have to say anything, but it may harm your defence if you do not mention when questioned something which you later rely on in court. Anything you do say may be given in evidence."

She looked up at Earle as a screech of tyres from the road outside screamed around the house.

Backup. Finally

Earle was holding a big pink duvet. From the top end, a riot of light-brown hair hung in rat's tails, and at the other end, red toenails peeked out. The lump in the middle, which he held against his chest, was weeping.

"Added to that list of arrests," Shona said, giving Mike an extra shove and being rewarded with a tortured moan. "The rape and murder of an as yet unknown female you confessed to, and the abduction of Tammy Robin."

"And *rape* of Tammy Robin," Earle said, his mouth downturning and his eyes narrowing. "Multiple."

"Jesus, you really are a sick son of a bitch, Mendes." Shona grabbed a handful of his thin hair and yanked it into her fist to keep his head still.

"I'll be d...dead...soon," he managed. "You...can't...lock me up...for long."

"No," she said, as two uniforms rushed in. "But your soul will burn in Hell for all eternity, and that's a really long fucking time."

Chapter Fifteen

"Hi, Ben, how has your day been?" Shona swung her chair away from desk and twirled left to right.

"Not bad, made a sale. Just on the way to KICKERS now."

"Great news on the sale." She paused. It was nice to hear his voice, soothing. It reminded her there were good people in the world. "But..."

"But you're not going to make it to the session tonight?"

"You've seen the news then."

"Yes, well done, seems like you stopped a madman in his tracks."

"Very mad, dangerous, too. But it means I'll be caught up at the station until late. There's things to wrap up, you know."

"Of course. How's the woman, the one who was missing?"

"Not good, but at least she's breathing. She's got another battle now, coming to terms with what happened, realising it's not her fault, and then rebuilding her life and her trust in men."

Ben was quiet for a moment. "You sound like you know what you're talking about."

"I...I've seen a few of these cases."

"It's disgusting how men abuse their physical power over women."

"Which is why I took up karate." She rushed on, not ready to divulge her past and how she knew what lay ahead for Tammy. "And I'm sorry about missing tonight. I know I was supposed to be taking the class as part of my grading."

"Plenty of time for all that. And I'm sorry, too."

"For what?"

"I said we'd go to the cinema on Saturday night, but my brother-in-law, he's having a bit of a freak out about becoming a father soon, and I said I'd go for a beer with him, talk it through, not that I have any experience of what he's got ahead, but you know, I like to be supportive."

"And you're very good at it. Listen, though, don't worry, some of the guys here are getting together in town for a drink on Saturday so

I'll join them. We decided it's time to stop meeting over corpses." She winced. She had to remember as an estate agent, Ben wasn't in the habit of discussing bodies and murder the way she was.

"Oh, okay." He cleared his throat. "Sounds like a good plan for you all. How about we go for a walk and a picnic on Sunday? If the weather holds, that is. Ealing Woods is nice."

"Not the woods." She squeezed the bridge of her nose and closed her eyes. Right now, there was an in-depth search going on for an as yet unnamed woman's body. "Perhaps we could drive to Wye Valley, that's nice, a bit more open."

"Good idea. I'll drop you a message Sunday morning."

"Perfect, see you then." She hung up and sighed as she looked out of the office window and over the car park. It was so easy with Ben. He put no pressure on her, it was casual, organic, their relationship natural and without complication. Which was exactly what she needed with the first man she'd allowed to get close after *that* night. And running a search on him—as Earle and Andy had suggested—interrogating him—which her father wanted to do—wasn't going to happen. She needed to get to know him the old-fashioned way, by talking, revealing bit by bit what was beneath the layers.

"Police surgeon report." Fletcher flapped a file in front of her. "On Mendes."

"Already? What's it say?"

Earle swung his chair to face them. His eyebrows raised.

"It's yours to read, but basically it says he's not fit for interview at the moment. He needs his pain bringing under control."

Shona glanced at Earle. She knew she'd thumped him pretty hard, but it had been self-defence, just the way it had been with Earle and Badger.

She could tell by Earle's eyes he was thinking the same thing.

"So he'll be assessed again, when he's undergone treatment," Fletcher said.

"He's not going to deny any of it," Shona said, "he confessed just before I arrested him. The three men he killed had all annoyed him in some minor way, and Tammy…"

"He just wanted a woman to abuse." Earle clenched his teeth and gripped the arms of his seat. "I thought she was dead when I first found her, it was hideous what he'd done. Took me a while to release the metal frame she was cuffed to, but I couldn't leave her, not for a second. She was sobbing my name over and over."

"She knows you?" Fletcher asked.

"Kind of. We investigated a gnome robbery at her mother's house," Earle replied. "And talking of gnome crime, uniform said they found a whole pile of what appeared to be smashed garden ornaments—gnomes—in Mendes' dining room."

"They did? What a weirdo." Shona tutted. "Honestly, I'll never understand some people."

"Some people you don't want to." Fletcher rested his hand gently on her shoulder. "Finish up as soon as you can. Get yourselves home. It's been one hell of a week…again."

"We will." Earle turned his wrist over and examined his watch. "But I can't see it being before ten."

"The price you pay for catching the bad guy is a mountain of paperwork." Fletcher shrugged. "But really well done, both of you. You're a great team, doing great work. It's not going unnoticed."

"Thanks, sir." Shona smiled. "We appreciate that."

* * * *

Shona walked into Aztec Pizza Parlour and glanced around for Earle. They'd agreed to meet before going to Grapes Ahoy. She'd used the excuse it saved Earle eating alone, but really she wanted to quiz him about Patrick and Badger. Now one case was closed, she had another on her mind.

Earle had said finding Tammy and catching the murderer were his priority, and they'd done that now. It was time to use her skills to find out what was going on with the small-time gangster who had a bee in his bonnet about her partner.

"Table for one?" a waiter asked, his eyeline dropping to the opening of her red silk blouse.

She'd teamed it with black leather trousers and scarlet stilettoes—after all, it was Saturday night.

"No, I'm meeting a friend here." She glanced around. "Actually, he's over there, by the window. Thank you."

"Can I bring you a drink?"

"A soda and lime would be great." She needed to hydrate before she hit Grapes Ahoy with the rest of the team. Likely the wine would be flowing once they left the pizza restaurant, and she hated waking on a Sunday with a wine headache.

Earle looked up from his phone as she approached. "Hey, partner."

She smiled. "All okay?"

"Yeah, successful day baking a chocolate and cherry mascarpone cake, I'm really pleased with it." He took a sip from his bottle of beer.

"Oh, do we get to eat it on Monday?" She sat.

"No. It's for a competition tomorrow in the town hall."

"Good luck with that. I've heard my mother say the judging is brutal."

"I won last year."

"You did?"

"Yes. Why are you surprised? You've tasted my cakes."

"I'm...not surprised. Just amazed how you find the time to do all of this baking."

"If I'm not at work, or at the gym, there's not much to do. I'm not a fan of TV, I'd rather be cooking and listening to music."

"What music?" She opened the menu but didn't drop her attention to it.

"Chopin, Debussy, Einaudi."

"Classical." One thing about Earle, he never failed to surprise her. She'd learnt not to let that show, though.

"Yeah, a bit of Strauss, too."

"Sounds like a perfect way to relax."

"It is."

The waiter appeared with her drink, and they ordered—Shona a small margarita, Earle a large meat feast. A side of garlic bread, too.

"So," Shona said, then took a deep breath. "What are we going to do about Badger?"

Earle stared out of the window at High Street. "It's getting busy out on the town."

"Don't change the subject."

He sighed. "Sorry, I'd just rather not think about Badger. And do I need to if he's in London?"

"That's the address he gave his parole board. What I want to know is why didn't Patrick call you?"

"I ignored several of his calls."

"Why?"

"I suppose…I suppose I wasn't ready to speak to him after…"

"After?"

"After it all happened and he transferred."

Shona wriggled on her seat, her leather trousers slippery. She was desperate to dig, to find out what happened, but that could bring a halt to the entire conversation, so she resisted. "Are you ready to speak to him now?"

"Perhaps."

"So do it." She linked her hands and leaned forward. "Here."

"Here?" he frowned.

"No time like the present." She nodded at the window.

A group of guys were wandering past, clearly a few beers already on board. On the opposite side of the street, a couple of bikers dressed all in black lurked in a doorway.

"If he's in Ironash and Patrick truly thinks he's a risk to you and had something to do with his shooting, we—"

"Need to know. I get that."

"So call him." She stood. "I'm going to nip to the ladies." She didn't really need to go, just wanted to give Earle a moment of privacy.

He nodded and pulled out his phone.

When she returned, lipstick fresh and hair brushed, he was still on the phone, listening.

She sat, rolling her lips in on themselves.

What has been said?

"Okay, thanks for the chat, keep getting better." Pause. "Goodbye, Patrick."

Shona didn't speak. There was something very definite about the goodbye.

Earle slipped his phone away, took a drink of beer, then wiped the back of his hand over his mouth.

"Well?" she asked.

"He's on the mend, like Fiona said. Frustrated that he can't get back to work sooner."

"He's a dedicated copper."

"Yeah, he is."

"Badger?"

Earle rubbed his right temple. "He thought he saw Badger that night, when bullets started flying about. Took him by surprise. Like me, he didn't know he was out. But his hair, it's distinctive."

"So you'd recognise him, too?"

"Absolutely." He studied High Street again as though scanning for the man in question. "Patrick was also frustrated that I hadn't been taking his calls, to warn me."

"Hence the letter."

"Yes, and as I thought Fiona was checking up on me." He paused. "But apparently it wasn't just..."

"What?"

"It wasn't just Badger's name Patrick was saying in his sleep, when he was high on pain meds. According to Fiona, he was also..."

Shona lowered her voice and leaned forward. "He was saying yours?"

"Yeah, but God knows why, it's not like...it's not like there was anything between us, ever."

"Fiona obviously doesn't think that's the case."

Earle pierced her with his gaze. "No, she wouldn't believe either of us. No matter what we said."

"But...and I hate to say this, but there's no smoke without fire, Earle."

"There was no fire, barely even a spark, because, hell, Patrick is married...to a woman. I kept my feelings for him under wraps, ignored them best I could, I'm a good guy. I didn't want to, and never want to, come between anyone. I'm not a homewrecker."

"So what happened?"

Will he finally tell me?

"Patrick he...he confessed one night, when we were on a stakeout, that he was confused. We'd been working together for two years, best friends on and off the job. We got on great, had so much in common."

Shona waited for him to go on.

"He told me he'd been thinking of *us* in a different way. He knew I was gay, I'd never hidden that from him, I'd even told him about a couple of dates I'd been on. Nothing came of either, by the way. So hearing him talk about us in a romantic sense when I'd been quashing any such thoughts for a long time threw me for a loop."

"What do you mean?"

"One minute I was angry, nothing could ever come of it, then I was hopeful; maybe he was the love of my life and it would all work out."

"So what happened?"

"Nothing, I wouldn't let it. Then he went and confessed to Fiona that he was feeling…what's the word he used…ah, yeah, curious, and I was the one who had made him feel that way." He paused. "The best way to describe her reaction was she hit the roof."

"Bloody hell."

"And I can't blame her. Patrick is her husband, they promised to be together until death parted them. She came into the station, late one night, luckily only Fletcher was there to hear her scream accusations at me. Vile, untrue accusations."

Shona shuddered. "That's awful."

"I told her she'd blown it all up out of proportion, but she wasn't having any of it. Eventually, she stormed out. The next day, Patrick asked Fletcher for a transfer."

"Manchester."

"Yeah, and he was gone by the end of the week." He shrugged. "That's why I was free for a partner when you showed up."

"And I feel lucky to have got you." She squeezed his hand. "Really I do. And I'm sorry you went through that. Sounds like you drew the short straw."

"It was certainly rough. Actually, no, more than that, it was a pile of shit. One of the reasons I didn't want to talk to him. There's never a good time to drag up old hurts, and I knew hearing his voice would do that."

"And how do you feel now, having spoken to him?"

"I'm glad he's okay, but he's history. Not that I don't wish him well, I do. But he needs to get better and live his life with Fiona. She'd always made him happy up until that point."

"And she can again?"

"Yeah, I'm sure of it. New town, new start."

"I hope they make it work." Shona paused as their pizzas were set down. When the waiter had walked away, she picked up her knife and fork. "I'm sorry, though, that you were left alone in all of this."

"But I'm not alone." He grinned suddenly. "I have you. The folk we're meeting in a few minutes down the road are also good people, friends. And I have my job, my aunt, my baking. I'm okay, really. Don't feel sorry."

"You'd like a special someone, though?"

"Of course, but I'm not looking for him. When the time is right, I'll know, and so will he."

Chapter Sixteen

By the time Shona and Earle had finished their pizza it was dark outside and they were late to meet Julie, Kyle, and Andy at Grapes Ahoy.

"We should hurry," Shona said when they stepped out into the cool night air.

"I don't think they'll be leaving the wine bar for a while, not once the Pinot is flowing." Earle glanced at the bikers.

The group had swollen to eight burly blokes. Most wore helmets, and there seemed to be some kind of heated discussion going on.

Shona glanced up at the CCTV camera over REVS. Hopefully it would be working, and the station would be keeping an eye on High Street.

As they made their way towards Grapes Ahoy, the voices behind them grew louder. A full-on argument was going on between the bikers. It wasn't clear what it was about, but tempers were flaring.

Shona glanced over her shoulder. They seemed to have split into two gangs. A couple of guys were rounding on each other, fists clenched.

"I should call it in," she said.

"Yeah." Earle took in the scene. "A few uniform here wouldn't hurt if they're going to kick off."

Suddenly, the shouting stopped. The air seemed to cease moving. The hairs on Shona's arms stood to attention, prickling against her silky blouse.

She turned once again.

Earle put his hand in the small of her back and pushed her forward. "Gun!"

"Shit." Her heart rate rocketed, and she broke into a stooped run in the opposite direction.

A shot rang out. Blasting around the high buildings, echoing over the pedestrianised street.

Another ear-splitting crack. This time the bullet hit the wall beside them, ricocheting off the brickwork and hitting a glass advertising screen holding a poster of cartoon animals. The glass shattered, scattering over the ground.

Shona ran faster, Earle at her side.

"Quick, in here." Earle opened the door to Grapes Ahoy. He slammed it, clicking the Yale lock into place so it was secure.

"Shit, is it Badger?" she gasped, snatching her phone from her pocket.

"Who knows." Earle was breathing fast as he looked up the street, his cheek pressed on the glass.

Her call was answered by the station. It wasn't Darren on the desk; a female officer greeted her calmly.

Shona didn't feel calm. Not by a long way. Her karate skills were no match for a bullet. "This is DI Williams, I'm on High Street, in Grapes Ahoy. There's a gang fight going on. Bikers. Shots have been fired, and we need armed backup. Now!"

"On it, ma'am."

"And tell them to hurry." Shona put her phone away and spun to the busy wine bar. She waved her hands in the air. "Police. Everyone out the back, move, move, move." The last thing she needed was bystanders getting hurt. "And make it sharp."

A collective wave of panic accompanied scraping chair legs and gasps of alarm. The swarm of people took off, shrinking into the shadows at the back of the long, thin room. A bright rectangle of light pierced the darkness as a fire door opened.

"Andy." Shona spotted him standing still, Julie and Kyle at his side. "Get out, now."

"What is it?" he called, his eyes wide.

"That bloke I asked you to search, Badger, he's out there...I think. You can't be here, and neither can they."

"I'm staying," Andy said.

"No, we've got it. Get out, and get the customers out. That's an order."

Andy hesitated, then he nodded and turned, directing the two SOCOs to the rear of the building along with a straggling bloke who looked ready to fight.

"Is it him?" Shona asked Earle.

"I'm not sure. They're not doing much, the bikers."

Shona strained to see, but no sooner had she focused, there was another shot.

She retreated, instinct pulling her away from the glass front of the wine bar. "Jesus, Earle, get back."

"I will, I…" He squatted, still peering out.

"Shona."

"Fuck." She spun around. "Ben. What are you doing here?" The rest of the bar area was empty now.

"I was having a drink with my brother-in-law." He gripped her shoulders, concern creasing his face. "What's going on? Was that a gunshot?"

"Yes. There's some loony out there with a firearm."

"Random?" Ben frowned and glanced at the door.

"I'm not sure." She shook her head. "Could be someone out to hurt my partner."

"Earle."

"Yes."

"Why?"

"Long story."

Ben frowned. "In that case, you need to get out of here, Shona." He tugged her deeper into the room, towards the exit door. "It's dangerous."

"I have to stay. I'm a police officer, Ben." She shrugged from his grip.

"And a damn good one, but if a madman is about to burst in here shooting, you have to leave...now."

"No. I have to—"

"Go, go, Shona." Earle stood. "Now...he's...he's...shit, he's coming this way." Earle backed up, stumbling into a table then scooting around it. "I'd recognise him anywhere."

"It's Badger?" Shona asked.

"Yeah...gun in one hand, walking stick in the other." He patted his side as if wishing he had a weapon holstered there.

"Come on," Ben said.

"I can't leave Earle."

"I'll stay with him."

"No, Ben!" The thought horrified her. What if something happened to Earle and Ben? How would she go on? She'd picked herself out of hell once before, she wouldn't be able to do it again. And losing these two wonderful men would definitely send her into her own private world of agony.

A shadow loomed at the door. Tall but stooped, a shard of light grazing his head, showing a strip of silver-grey winging over an otherwise black full head of hair.

"Fuck," Earle muttered, backing up farther.

"He's got a gun," Ben said, "we need to get out of here."

"Keep going," Earle said, retreating.

"Is help on the way?" Ben asked.

"Yes," Shona said, "but who knows how long it will take to get the armed response here."

"Get down!" Earle yelled. He rushed behind the end of the bar and hunched into a ball.

Ben dropped to the floor behind a big wine barrel tipped on its end to serve as a table. Shona went with him.

A shot tore around the bar, instantly followed by the tinkle of glass breaking and landing on the hard tiled floor.

"He's in," Shona said in a hushed whisper. She had to fight to keep the panic at bay. Her stomach was a tight fist of fear.

Ben gulped, then his jaw set hard in a way she hadn't seen before. It was as if he were gathering his energy and determination.

"Montague, you piece of shit, I know you're in here." A thick, deep voice echoed around the bar.

Another shot, to the right this time. It hit the optics. More glass exploding then chinking to the floor in a waterfall.

"You really think you can hide?" Badger shouted. "That you won't pay for what you did to me?"

Shona peered around the wine barrel she was using as a shield.

Badger was crunching through the glass, walking past the long edge of the bar that had plastic grapes hanging from fake vines overhead. His gun was pointing downwards at his side in an unnervingly casual manner, as if this wasn't something new to him, to be stalking a police officer and shooting a place up.

"I've got to do something," Shona whispered to Ben.

"Like what?" He glanced at the rear door. "I don't think we can make a run for it, we need to wait until he's close enough so we can disarm him."

"I agree. But I can't let him see Earle, he'll shoot him on sight."

"He might not."

"He shot Earle's previous partner, he tried to kill him."

"Fuck," Ben muttered, rubbing his forehead. "Why?"

"Because he's a psycho with a grudge."

Badger reached the end of the bar.

Earle shrank into the shadows.

"Backup will be here soon, Ben" she said. "Have faith."

"What? What are you doing?"

"This." Shona stood, arms raised. "Don't shoot."

"Bloody hell, Shona." Ben reached for her leg.

She stepped away from him, away from the barrel. "What do you want?"

Badger settled his attention on her. "Ah, I know you, don't I."

Good. Look this way.

"Yeah, you're Montague's bitch, right." He sneered.

"Why are you here, Badger?"

"Wow, you know who I am. You're sexy and smart. Shame he's a queer." Badger laughed. His top two front teeth were missing. "Won't ever get a go at you." With his free hand, he cupped his groin. "I wouldn't mind some, though."

"If you know who I am, you also know I'm a police officer." She tilted her chin, tried to project authority. "You need to put down your weapon."

"And why would I do that? I haven't finished with it." He waved it left to right.

She braced. "You have to if you don't want to go back to prison for a very long time."

"Prison doesn't scare me. In fact, I couldn't give a fuck."

"You can't mean that."

"Yeah, I can. What I'm interested in is revenge. Getting the bastards who snapped my spine in half. One down, one to go."

"It was an accident," she said. "From what I heard, there was no undue force used."

"Ha, they fucking tell you that? 'Course they did."

"You have a condition." She was trying desperately to keep the quiver from her voice when all she could concentrate on was the wrong end of a gun. "And if you hadn't been brandishing a broken bottle, there'd have been no need to subdue you."

"Might have known you'd be on his side." He took a step closer but was still too far away for a take out. He'd shoot before she could get to him and whip his legs from beneath him. "And where'd he go, that Montague fella. I saw his ugly mug just outside a fucking minute ago."

"He went out the back, before you came in," she said.

Badger frowned and glanced around.

Shona kept her attention on Badger's face, knowing if she looked at the dark corner, she'd give Earle away.

"What the fuck." Badger frowned and he peered over her shoulder. "Where'd he go? Through there?"

"I don't know. I told him to make a sharp exit, and he did."

"And he just left you? Knowing you'd be alone with me?" Badger laughed. "It's fucking unreal that everyone puts him on a pedestal. He's an arsehole. But as he's not here, why don't you bend over that barrel there." He held up the gun. "No point wasting this trip out and the help of my mates to get in here."

Shona opened her mouth to tell him where to go, but before she had time to speak, Ben was in front of her, and all she could see was the back of his broad shoulders.

"You won't lay a finger on her."

"Oh no?" Badger raised his eyebrows. "And who the fuck are you?"

"Ben." Shona put her hands on his shoulders and went to step around him, but he blocked her, keeping her shielded.

"Just a member of the public who won't watch a prick hurt a woman."

"You think I'm a prick, huh. Well, bad news for you, I'm a prick with a gun and I'm feeling horny." He raised the weapon, the dark hole of the barrel winking their way.

"Oh God." Shona gasped.

Ben tensed but stayed rooted to the spot.

"Come on, I won't say it again." Badger took a step closer, waving the gun manically.

"No. It's me you want." Earle stood, his tall frame unfolding from the shadows.

Badger stepped backwards, two quick paces so he could see all three of them. His eyes widened, and a sickening smile balled his cheeks. "Ah, there you are, arsehole. And yeah, it's you I want but I kind of want her, too." He laughed sickeningly. "Maybe you and the hero over there can both watch while I have my end away."

A red rage flooded Shona. Her hate for this man was suddenly all-consuming. Her body ached with the need to fight, to hurt, to get him down and keep him down.

But still Ben shielded her.

"Leave her alone. Let them both go and you can have me." Earle tapped his chest. "Free shot."

"Earle, no!" Shona shouted. Why the hell was he goading this madman?

Earle glanced her way, then over her shoulder.

She spun, following his line of sight.

The fire escape door was no longer lit from the white bulb in the corridor beyond. It was in darkness which, for Shona, meant one thing. Help had arrived.

She tugged Ben and took a step backwards.

He came with her, but his attention didn't leave Badger.

"You know I want you to suffer, to have a long, slow, and painful death," Badger said to Earle. "And all the while you can think what a fucking sorry excuse for a police officer you are. How really you're just a black fucking queer who doesn't deserve to live."

Earle said nothing, though his eyes flashed. He was raging inside but holding it in.

A shuffle behind, softer than soft footsteps.

"Any last words?" Badger sneered. "Before I kill you, then him…" He swung the gun Ben and Shona's way. "And fuck her."

"My last words?" Earle said. He folded his arms, puffed up his chest, and nodded at Badger's black jacket. "How about it's time for you to give it up. Because you, Udall Hicks, are under arrest for—"

"Shit! Fuck!" Badger retreated. His shoulders bumped into the wall as he stared down at the four red dots dancing on his leather jacket.

He couldn't see the red pinpoint set solid between his eyes. "What the?" He swiped at his chest, trying to brush the targets from him. The gun was swinging around wildly.

"Armed police. You are surrounded. Drop the weapon," a loud, firm voice bellowed from Shona's right. "Now."

"What? Fuck." Badger threw his gun to the floor. It fired. A sudden flash and a cracking bang. A stool leg splintered, shards of wood exploding into the air.

"On your knees!" Earle stepped forward.

"Fuck!" Badger dropped to his knees, landing lopsided. "Shit. Call them off. Call them off." He held his hands up, cactus-like, and shook as he still looked at the targets on his torso.

"This way." Ben spun and caught Shona in his arms.

"No, I can't, I—"

"Get out of here," an armed officer threw their way. Then, with his weapon raised and poised on Badger, he slunk forwards and stood next to Earle.

Another officer grabbed Badger's discarded weapon then backed up, his black outfit melting him into the shadows. His red target never left Badger's head.

"Wait." Shona held Ben's arm. "Earle needs a witness for this arrest."

"There's plenty of witnesses."

"I want to."

Ben stilled, though she sensed it was with reluctance.

"Udall Hicks." Earle took a pair of cuffs from the officer next to him, "you are under arrest for the illegal possession of a firearm, firing of that weapon in a public place, destruction of property, for the attempted murder of DI Patrick Marlborough, and threatening a police officer. You do not have to say anything, but it may harm your defence if you do not mention when questioned something which you later rely on in court. Anything you do say may be given in evidence."

Earle clasped the cuffs into place then nodded at two armed officers. "Take him away."

Blocking a leg attack wasn't likely, given their height difference. It would be easier for him to aim for her face or throat.

Backup. I could really do with you right now.

"He wouldn't give me codeine, when my liver hurt." Mendes rubbed below his ribs with his free hand. The same spot he'd indicated when in Mrs Robin's kitchen. "Would only have taken him a minute to get me some, but did he care about me being in pain? Did he fuck. He just wanted to piss off home for his dinner."

"He was a diabetic, his dinner was important for his own health."

Mike was quiet for a few seconds, then, "Well, it's not anymore."

A loud creak on the stairs. A woman crying in short squeaking sobs. Earle speaking, soft and soothing.

Time seemed to halt. Shona was aware of the breath whooshing in and out of her lungs, her pulse pounding in her ears.

If there was any doubt in her mind that Earle had found Tammy Robin, it vanished.

Mike sprang forwards, knife extended, an ugly snarl twisting his features.

Shona crouched and flung her left arm up, blocking the knife by stopping the downward thrust of Mike's forearm. Immediately, she hopped to the left, hurling a sternal punch his way because she wasn't sure how much power she could get into a high face hit.

"Bitch," he huffed, chasing after her instantly, knife still at the ready.

It's as if I didn't touch him.

And she knew damn well she had a good pack with her punch.

He stabbed at her again.

This time she knocked it sideways with a well-practiced move she could do in her sleep. The blade flashed in a ray of sunlight pouring through the window. She hoped it would go skittering, but it didn't.

In a second he was going for her again, a gut strike this time.

Chapter Seventeen

"And now I'm taking you away." Ben kept his arm wrapped around Shona's waist and ushered her through the exit.

Within minutes, she found herself standing in the corner of the garden at the rear of Grapes Ahoy. In the near darkness stood wooden tables and benches and wine barrels transformed into colourful planters. A fence shielded them from the Armed Response Unit.

She gulped in the cool air, glad of the way it stroked her throat, but it didn't dampen down her acute irritation. "What the hell do you think you're doing, Ben?" She stepped away from him and rammed her hands on her hips.

"The bad guy had been arrested, it was time to get away from all those guns."

"No, not that…" She pointed back the way they'd just come. "Being *there*. I ordered the place to empty."

A neat line forged between his eyebrows. "You really think I'd leave you with a madman?"

"Yes."

"No way."

"Yes, because I told you to."

He rubbed his chin and looked at her. With only the light of the moon on his face, it would have been easy for Shona to get distracted by just how handsome he was…but she didn't.

"Ben," she said. "That was dangerous staying behind. And what you did, standing in front of me."

"Was exactly what I should have done."

"Not in the eyes of the law. If he'd shot, if he'd shot you…" She shook her head. "A civilian caught in the line of fire is a nightmare."

"Nightmare or not, it was instinct."

"Not exactly a self-preservation instinct." Her heart was going like the clappers, adrenaline still being used up even though everything was calm now. "Bloody hell."

"Shona."

"What?"

"I care about you, you're special to me, but I like to think I would have done the same for anyone." He paused. "And for a while I wasn't sure if I was the sort of man who would."

She let her arms fall to her sides. "What do you mean, Ben?"

"For a while I had little to be proud of, I'd..." He dropped his gaze to the floor and slid his hands into his jeans pockets.

"Ben?"

He sighed. "I've been meaning to talk to you..."

"About what?"

"Fuck." He turned away.

Shona glanced to her right. Behind the fence, the armed officers were taking Badger to the meat wagon. Earle's deep voice joined in with the others. He was taking control. Good, she didn't need to get involved.

"Ben." She set her attention on him again. In all their dates, she'd never seen him anything but open and confident. "What is it?"

He sat on one of the benches, gripping the wood either side of his legs.

"Ben, what do you mean you had little to be proud of?"

"You probably know already." He shrugged. "When you did a police record search on me."

"A police record search?" She shook her head. "Why would I do that?"

"Why wouldn't you? You have access to everyone's files."

"But that would be an abuse of my position, Ben."

He raised his eyebrows. "So you haven't?"

"No." She sat next to him. "Why? What is it?"

What the hell has he done?

He pursed his lips and blew out a breath. Closed his eyes for a long moment then opened them. "You know I said we moved here from Yorkshire."

"Yes, I remember."

"It was because of me. Because of me my family didn't want to stay there."

Shona was quiet, waiting for him to go on.

"There were these lads, troublemakers. I hung out with them, the wrong crowd my mother always said. But they were a laugh and they relieved the boredom of the empty evenings. There was nothing to do in our town, no youth club, and the gym and cinema were expensive. So I just, well, loitered around street corners."

"I get that."

He shrugged. "They got into a bit of petty theft, taking what they wanted from the local shops as long as they could hide it in a jacket."

Shona was quiet.

"But they got more daring." His hands tightened on the bench.

Shona sat next to him, covered his left knuckles with her palm. "Go on."

"One day they decided it would be a good idea to take what was in the till. A young guy was at the front of the shop, nerdy, an easy target. Using plastic guns from Toys R Us, we held the place up. Cam, he was the brains behind our antics, ordered the money to be put in a bag. We legged it then, wearing Shaun the Sheep masks."

"And how long did it take for the police to come knocking?"

"Less that twenty-four hours. It was an idiot thing to do. The worst. That poor bloke, we scared him silly, and all for eighty quid. I hated myself."

"People make mistakes." She studied his profile, trying to imagine him as a reckless, impressionable teen capable of such a huge lapse in judgement.

"You're kind. That was one hell of a mistake." He turned to her. "You sure you didn't know about it already?"

"First I've heard of it. You, like everyone else, is entitled to privacy."

"Thanks. I know it looks bloody awful on paper, what I did, and the sentence I got in young offenders." He turned his hand over and wrapped his fingers around hers. "You can leave now if you want."

"Why would I want to?"

"You're a police officer, a fine upstanding member of society, why would you want to be with me?"

"Oh, Ben." She smiled softly. "I prefer to judge you for how I see you now, for how you treat me and make me feel."

"Which is?"

"Safe, appreciated, happy."

"I like those words." He managed a half-smile. "If it hadn't been for my uncle giving me a chance in his business, then I don't know if I would have ever got work."

"But he did, and you have a good job, not to mention KICKERS. That's no small feat to get a club up and running."

"Thank you, karate saved me. I wanted that opportunity to be there for others. Teens in particular." He inclined his head, then reached out and tucked a strand of hair behind her ear. "So you'll still come out with me, tomorrow?"

"Yes. Of course."

"You don't hate me?"

"No, Ben. I don't think I could ever hate you." She leaned forward and brushed her lips over his.

He cupped her cheek and looked into her eyes. "And one day, Shona."

"Yes."

"You'll tell me about your past?"

She swallowed, waiting for the familiar dark tightening of her chest when she thought of *that* night. But it didn't come. Her stomach didn't sink. Her skin didn't prickle.

"When you're ready," he said softly. "No rush."

"Thank you." She held his gaze. "I'm not ready to yet, and that's nothing personal, but I will."

"Like I said, no rush." He pulled her in for a kiss then wrapped his arms around her.

She sank against him, breathing in his cologne and enjoying the strong, secure embrace. A sensation of letting go, relaxing, being cared for washed over her.

She didn't have to be tough all the time, and Ben seemed to understand that. It had taken her years to even think about dating, about letting someone in again, but Ben, he was undoing the bolts to her heart one at a time. Maybe she'd be able to learn from him how to put the past into the history books, where it belonged.

ABOUT IRONASH

Ironash is a fictional town in the heart of England, now kept safer by the return of DI Shona Williams. And it's just as well, a lot of bad shit happens there!

#1 Sin, Repent, Repeat
#2 The Last Post
#3 Blind Panic
#4 Bucket List

Follow A. J. Harlem on AMAZON to get an alert when new books are released in the IRONASH series.

Website ajharlem@weebly.com

About the Author

A. J. Harlem is a bestselling author who has opened her vivid imagination to create thrilling British detective novels. She's always lived in the UK —England, Scotland, and currently South Wales—and adores the colloquial use of the English language and quintessential settings for murder, crime, and high drama. When she isn't writing, her favourite pastimes generally revolve around her love of animals and include horse riding on the beach, walking her dogs in the Welsh mountains, and flying birds of prey.